TYRO

·

the lives of Q

·

LAURIE EVAN OWEN

Matador
Unit E2 Airfield Business Park,
Harrison Road, Market Harborough,
Leicestershire. LE16 7UL
Tel: 0116 2792299
Email: books@troubador.co.uk
Web: www.troubador.co.uk/matador
Twitter: @matadorbooks

ISBN 978 1805140 825

British Library Cataloguing in Publication Data.
A catalogue record for this book is available from the British Library.

Printed and bound in the UK by TJ Books Limited, Padstow, Cornwall

Typeset in 12pt Adobe Garamond Pro by Troubador Publishing Ltd, Leicester, UK

Matador is an imprint of Troubador Publishing Ltd

**Dedicated to the memory of Ben Owen,
the author's father, a shy, kindly man who in no way
resembled any of the characters depicted herein.**

·

Acknowledgements

For their invaluable support and friendship during and after
the writing of this book, the author would like to thank the
following:

Thomas H Green –
Music journalist, and co-founder of *theartsdesk.com*

Maggie Brookes-Butt –
Poet/novelist and former BBC producer.
Author of the novels *The Prisoner's Wife* (2020)
and *Acts of Love and War* (2022).

Lindy Foster Weinreb –
Designer, founder of Bridgwater Boats and former director
of *DeeTV.tv*.

Dick Douglass –
Film director (*Hamlet* 2017), writer, actor and musician.

Of all earth's meteors, here at least is the most strange and consoling: that this ennobled lemur, this hair-crowned bubble of the dust, this inheritor of a few years and sorrows, should yet deny himself his rare delights, and add to his frequent pains, and live for an ideal, however misconceived.

Robert Louis Stevenson : from the essay 'Pulvis Et Umbra'

I died for Beauty – but was scarce
Adjusted in the Tomb
When One who died for Truth, was lain
In an adjoining Room –

He questioned softly 'Why I failed'?
'For Beauty', I replied –
'And I for Truth – Themself are One –
'We Brethren, are', He said –

And so, as Kinsmen, met a night –
We talked between the Rooms –
Until the Moss had reached our lips –
And covered up – our names –

Emily Dickinson : poem no. 449

...the lives...

- Allégories. – Rèveries. Singulière situation de l'homme !
Sujet intarissable. Produire, produire !

Journal of Eugène Delacroix : 27 March 1824

TYRO

·

the lives of Q

·

1.   Soho

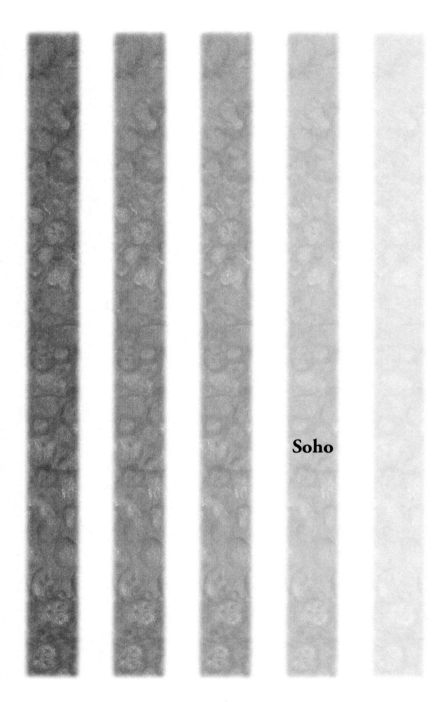

Soho

How does it feel

the gravity of blood and stone
the presence of air
hollow ground

the subject

Q

Broke white
floodlit flakes of it
dropping to nothing.

Snow and more snow,
lingering not even for a heartbeat on
the headless cold corpse of a Soho pigeon,
still in the gutter, where it was yesterday,
was yesterday,
yesterday.

Opposite.
Dom's Diner.
All-Day Breakfast.
On Special Offer.

Squatting legs akimbo on a window barstool
the scrawny wraith of Eugène Delacroix
prinks the brim of a dimpled fedora.

On the adjacent barstool
his youthful companion refocuses on the grizzled cadaver,
strokes the scab from a day-old neckspot and impels the point
of his 2H Staedler drawing pencil to a harder sharper serif as
definitive elucidation of the zigzaggy purple wingtip stretched
out so conveniently across the granite kerb.

Eugène bestows
an approving grin.
Doffs the fedora.
Drifts. Dilutes.
Fades.

Beyond the wet tarmac.
Beyond the headless pigeon and the double yellow lines and
cracked yorkstone slabs, the oval windows of the *Pink'n Pert
Eroticorium* inhabit their own kind of self-regarding mustard
glow, excommunicated from all other illumination, repelled
by the gentle come-hither of the falling flakes.

Out of.
Out of the February night.
A glossy black Bentley with a left hand drive
draws up to park its crude silhouette
before the sex shop.

The driver
clambers out.

Familiar. Lop-sided.
Scurries over the narrow pavement.
Disappears into the Victorian terrace
through a heavy mudbrown door.

All this while.
In the Bentley's rear.
Sharp, colossal and dark
against the glowering mustard of the sex shop's middle
window sits a lumpish ideogram of minatory bulk, crowned
either by an xl glengarry or a mountainous quiff
of jocular belligerence.

*   *   *

Back
in Dom's Diner,
the 23-year-old artist
blinks.

Lays down his pencil.

Leans forward.

Inspects
the number plate.

2.

Cabaret

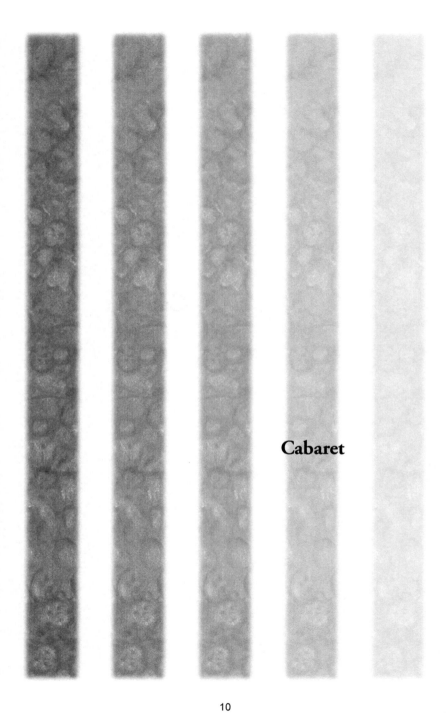

Cabaret

Q.
Artist. Tyro.
Coerces the door.
Ascends the stairs.

Walled in, right
and left. Ducted
through a stinking
glitzy gloom-laid calyx.

Ascends the gradient.
The jewelled staircase.

Lifts his feet.
From radiation days.
From holes hacked out
by pleated primogenitors.

Lifts his feet.
From spatchcock magpies
hooked on boneposts round
the rim of superstition wood.

Climbs each
knuckled nosing,
creaky tread and riser.

Light-emitting diode clumps
of amber, amethyst and stale carnelian
underhang in tubes the lip of each oak tread.

He climbs. And climbs.
His leading foot scales the diminished height of the final riser, dropping with an unpleasant slap on the bare boards of the landing. He steps and stumbles into another heavy door which grates open onto a space even darker than the stairwell. But warmer. Much warmer.

A chest-high orange spotlight squints through the murk, picking out a bentwood kitchen chair with a frayed cane seat. Scattered on the floor around the chair lies a motley of coloured wigs. In a psychedelic take on what he flags as bolshie bluesman Bukka White's *Fixin' to Die*, the sunken distant tones of a baritone sax rumble round the room.

The door hisses shut. Behind him.
He scuffles away from it. Backwards,
into a wall. Sideways, into a corner.

One of the wigs, a mousy close-cropped pageboy, appears to wriggle and skip a couple of inches. He looks harder. Definitely moving. Being twitched from side to side by a polished black combat boot connected to the wrinkly phosphorescent side-stripe of a track-suited human shank.

Semi-circling the spotlit performance area are three rows of kitchen chairs, also cane-seated, but with cushioned headrests. Some are occupied. Most are not.
The audience is widely and evenly dispersed.
The pale and vaguely male faces dangle
suspended from an astral penumbra.

A dozen. Immobile. Or slowly
orbiting. Sluggish.
Dead moons.

His eyes are still adjusting to the murk when from behind an antique canvas screen in the far corner of the chamber emerges a slender, graceful, entirely bald but unmistakably female presence. Moving into the spotlight. Not young. Not old. Disconcertingly at ease, in a shimmering,
floor-length dressing gown of burgundy satin.
She glides over to the central chair.
Sits down.

Her arrival causes a marked
but short-lived kerfuffle
in the small assembly.

The scalp and face of the charismatic duenna are of a cold ceramic whiteness. The green eyes are wide and musty like huge melon-seeds. The sadistic knife-slash of her mouth lies in wait beneath a hard little nose constructed of three melded triangles. She is studying the members of her congregation, all cowering behind flesh-coloured half-masks, sliced-off, straight across, just below the cheekbone.

Something like a smile is softening the cruel slit of her lips. At the same time her robe slithers open to disclose the entirety of an immaculate slender leg and an equally immaculate slender foot garbed in a golden sandal. Continuing her unhurried perusal of the masked brethren, who remain static as undertakers, she gives no sign of having noticed Q. Pressed back. As he is.
In his corner.

Slowly. Very slowly. She bends forward. Holding her gown together with one hand, she reaches down with the other to select from the wigs around her feet an elaborate straw-blonde pompadour. Placing it on her lap, she caresses into place one of the more wayward curls before lifting and lowering the whole sculpted artefact onto her hairless head.

At this point some of the men at the rear grow nervous. Start fidgeting with their masks. Working and burrowing their heads as far back as possible into the plush headrests. Tap-tapping on their cane seats. Plucking at the rattan strips bound around each and every hoop of thick bamboo.

Her attention however
is focussed within. On herself.
She stands. Turns her neck. Rolls her thorax.
A somnolent tigress. Uncurling.
Stretching.
Arising.

And as she rises,
the satin gown sags from her shoulders and slips to the floor.
Apart from the wig, a lacy gold thong and the gold sandals,
she is naked. More than naked. Unbreathing. Nothing to
disturb the meagre but agreeably adequate disposition of taut
white flesh on her younger-than-it-should-be body. Wig.
Thong. Sandals. Something else. In her right hand. Pointing
down. Next to her thigh. Something long. Shiny. Complex.
Her eyes are staring straight ahead,
at one of the punters in the back row.
The arm cantilevers up, forward.
On its pristine hinge.

The thing in her hand
is a long black pistol
with a steel silencer.

Someone coughs.
A chair spasms.
Jerks back.

The tyro
has had enough.
He lurches forward, eyes down and half-shut.
Accelerates across the room toward the canvas screen.
Brushing past the immobile shootist. Barely noticing the
overpoweringly fructose aroma
of honey and bearded iris.

At the screen, he trips, slips on a wig.
Overbalancing but somehow managing not to fall. Behind
the screen. Another door. Pushes down on the catch lever.
Wrenches it open. Walks into coldness. Blackness.

With a frantic hand he reaches out behind him to prevent the
door from slamming and blocking out the thin sliver of light
from the auditorium.

Too late.
Slam. Click-click.
Blackness. Cold. Utter blackness.

Fingertips outstretched,
straining forwards and sideways,
find nothing, not before, nor to the side,
nor behind, not even the door he has just come through.

No further.

Wait.

For his eyes, to adapt.

But his right foot is in the air. Descending in anticipation.

Ready to anchor his centre of gravity to the spot.

Any spot.

His left leg, shaking. His right foot, still in limbo,
hovers and lowers. Seeks but finds nothing.

Nowhere to land.

Hands clutch.

Body sways.

Tilts. Tumbles.

Capsizes arsy-versy.

Shrinks.

To a ball.

  A rolling ball.

    A ball of bone and bark.

      A broken, boxy, cartwheeling ball.

        And just as his cheek is slapped

          by an iron-hard slimy dado and

            his tibia shattered by a stair edge,

          snapping his calf into his crotch,

        and just as his elbow is clattered

by another slimy dado, and just as every adamantine rim

and every weaponed corner of this pitching black universe

is bludgeoning into him without pity, so he attempts to slow
his momentum by throwing out all of his limbs in the same
straight direction,
which turns,
bounces,
flattens him,
into a face-down
nose-diving toboggan,
so that every cut of his carcass
seems spanked and slashed and cudgelled
by the avenging cranky knuckles of every stair.

He spreads and angles his feet.
Kicking them out, down
and hard, for brakes.

But the gradient is too steep.
Only when his outreaching hands
are torqued and crushed by the concrete floor
does his beaten body crumple and slump
into semi-consciousness.

Wet.

Ice-cold.
Basalt-black.

A bruise.

Of mash and gristle.

Marooned. In a polar bog.

Mid all the hurt.

All the starry myopia.

All the hurtling diacritics.

He shifts his cloven bones.

Armless hands.

Legless feet.

Kneels. Reels. Squats.

A door rattles

against his crombie.

He drags himself upright.

Dazed. Dizzy. Out of everything.

Leans on the door.

Grabs at rusted bolts, splintery mouldings. Feels for a light
switch on the walls. Finds one. It doesn't work. Slithers his
fingers over the door. Finds a dimpled brass knob, which he
manages to turn using both hands. An interior lever clicks.
The door loosens. Opens inwards. A thread of streetlight.

Readjust. Restore. Balance.

Walk.

Outside.
A dimly lit cul-de-sac.
Off Matte Way. Off Old Compton.

Sleet.
Morphing to rain.

Checks his face, his scalp, for bleeding.
Smoothes his hair with his ripped-up hands.

Straightens his clothes.
Shoulders his bag.

Back in traffic.
Under a sodium sky.

Scans his mobile.

2am.

3.   Fitzrovia

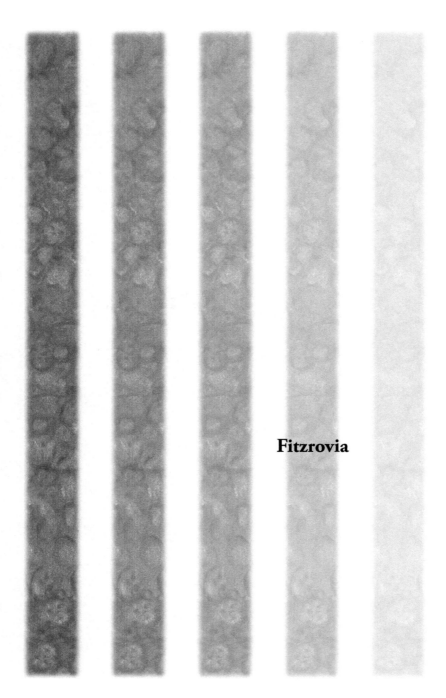

Fitzrovia

Rain.

And sleet.

And rain again.

Old Compton.

Rain and more rain.

Shovelling, rip-roaring down in a clattery

ubiquitous, neverending subhuman retch.

He stops. Curses.

Lets it pour all over him.

Turns left. Splashes and hobbles his way up Charing Cross Road. Takes shelter in a coffee shop doorway. Remembers his beret and sketchbook buried in a deep outer pouch of his crombie. Transfers sketchbook to his manbag and the beret to his dripping head. Decides. Embark on the stormy hike home. But in discrete hyperdynamic chunks.

Chunk one. To Goodge Street.

Into the rain. Once more. North. Past the Tube Station. Across the main road. On and on through worldwars of wetness. Ezrapounded by a nazi blitzkrieg of ten gallon ice tanks, by self-multiplying frost-filled blister-bombs and roiling bombardments of hate and hail and hyperthermia.

On. And on.

Through squalling bathloads of uber-arctic mickey bliss. Punting his sodden dogs up the spate of Tottenham Court Road. His manbag pummelling the backs of his thighs under the scant protection of his drenched crombie.

On past Boots. Waterstone's. Poundland.

Past the Moroccan kebab shop.

Air-blasted, laminated
to the blind granitic cliff
of Fitzrovia Police Station,
the glacial waters pitch down
in five-storey diaphanous slabs.
He ratchets forward. Through the deluge.
Comes at long last to his first stop. The sheltered colonnade of a row of electronics and computer stores. In a well-lit deep-set doorway he perches on a narrow windowsill.
Squeegees drops of blood and rain from his hair.
Wrings muddy puddles from his beret,
his coat and his trouser bottoms.

Through a gap under the shop door his ankles feel a warm breath of remission, a hint of something better. Shuffles away from the howling and clashing. Huddled in his hole. Works and reworks the muscles all over his body.

Gives himself twenty minutes.

Eugène enters. Sits. Beside him.
Blowing his hands, stamping his feet.
Dispensing his genial wink.

And then gone.
Just as another friendly face
floats in from the tempest.
Izzy Higgs.

'Who ordered this ?'
Isidor Isaac Higgs drops into the place vacated by Eugène.
Opens a polystyrene takeaway box and peers tetchily at the
steaming sauce-swamped heap of nourishment tucked into
a beige pitta envelope. 'Looks like donner to me. Ordered
shish'n they gave me fuckin donner. Here you are matey.
Can't fuckin stand donner.' He shoves it at Q, who takes it
with shivering hands and a nod of thanks.

The arrival is burly. Red-faced. Impregnable.
Dressed in a high-collared Russian army coat under a battle-
scarred cossack hat with the flaps down, neither of which
seems particularly wet, he takes a fag from a packet of
Gauloises Brunes and lights up to enjoy the sight of his half-
drowned companion demolishing the jilted kebab. 'Just been
here,' he says, pulling from his coat a postcard-size ticket for
what appears to be some kind of alt-cabaret allnighter. 'Why
don't you go? It's only round the corner in the old GCHQ

building. I was there for a while and it's not bad. The card's got my name on it so they'll let you in. Be a chance to warm up and dry out. Might even be some free booze left. Take it. You're very welcome,' he grunts. Q takes the ticket with kebab-filled gratitude.

Izzy chokes the life out of his cigarette. 'Anyway. Where the hell you been, to get beaten up and soaked through like that? Haven't seen you for ages. You still at the Schools ?'

Shrugging his shoulders, mumbling an indecipherable response to the well-meant enquiry, he shepherds a noncommittal grin into his weary mouth.

'Righto matey,' exhales the visitor, 'gotta go,' jumping to his feet and scooting off round the storefront corner.

In the young artist's ripped fingers the woolly oblong of the ersatz complimentary ticket feels benign,
oddly agreeable,

its navy letters
lifting, and blurring,
from their greygreen field…

'Les Futons Infernaux'

4.   *G C H Q*

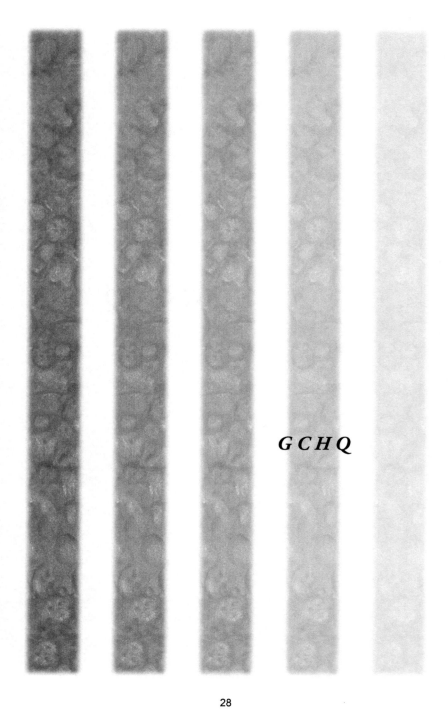

G C H Q

Go   ment
Com   ications
He   arters

Man-
handling
bromidic gears
through the plate-glass whirligig,
through the brute carpet of severed legs
and heads. Through the deafmute dreary fog.

He activates
his phonetorch.
Struggles on. Another metre.
Puts his finger to the big red button.

The travellator
discharges a snort.
Grumbles into its shift.

Tines of pewter,
geysering up from some lower hemisphere,
pour forth in flat ribbons. Drawn to the tacky black plastic of
the handrail, he is yanked importunately forward, onto the
torrent of grey metal.

Still cold,
even moribund,
he doesn't need to walk.
His wet boots, uptilted by the glum machine,
are transported. Up. Up and up.
Up through the purples
of the veiling mist.
He disembarks.

Warmth. Cossetted in gloom, he follows a trail of grubby white chevrons stuck to the geriatric varnish of the parquet floor, all the way to a curtain of mottled aubergine velvet. Which is drawn aside. To let him in.

A low-lit hangar.
Hundreds of red leather futons. All crammed together in semicircular rows around a synthetic mechanoid playpark, which is itself chocabloc with identical greygreen boulders and colossally formalised pink-and-crimson trees.

The park extends for at least an acre.
The floor is tiled with slabs of loganberry jasper. The walls are for the most part hidden by the enormous trees and fake boulders. The ceiling is invisible through the gloom. Every futon but one, in the front row, is occupied singly by an uncomfortable mix of gender, age and ethnicity.

He is handed a glass of red wine. Sits on the empty futon.

Above his head flickers a screen.

Of jittery runes:

::: ::: *LES FUTONS INFERNAUX* ::: :::

: 17 :

' LE VER BLANC '

In the furthest, darkest,

reaches of the arena. A disturbance. Between the trees.

A pale cloud glimmers into focus, accompanied by a sickly-sweet, intermittent stench. The cloud appears to solidify into a vast, opaline sausage or dog-turd. But then it moves.

A grotesquely bloated, elephantine maggot perhaps.

Or Bram Stoker's White Worm.

The body is sleek.

Burnished. Aerodynamic like a high speed train.

Overcoated in creamy vermiform ripples. And without end.

Its tiny whale eyes and gargantuan mouth open and close in time to staved tumults of inrushing/outrushing air.

Its myriad teeth are gold and short and sharp.

Its tongue is rough, fetid and orange.

Slithering closer all the time, the creature slows,
stopping five metres from the nearest futon,
which holds Q,
petrified.

The mouth opens.
From its oesophagus.
A hoarse, guttural
idiolect…

'Flōðe blōðe peōl — fōle tō ræʒōn —
hātan heolfpe. Þopn ſtundum ſonʒ
fūrlic pynd-leoð. Fēþa eal ʒeſæt.'

Torpid and deliberate.
A markedly formal peroration.
The invertebrate mollusc closes its mouth,
unfurling its lips to allow the excretion of its mammalian
tongue. Q observes the pulse. Thumping like a trapped pig
below the greasy stinking tip. The orange proboscis writhes
this way and that. In lascivious pretzels. Testing the air.
Returns to its throat.

More rasps.

More snarls.

Deep. Bubbled. Breathings.

The mouth closes.

Re-opens…

'ᵹeꞅāƿon ðā æꝼꞇeꞃ ƿæꞇeꞃe ƿýꞃm-cýnneꞅ ꝼela

ꞅellīce ꞅæ-ðꞃacan ꞅunð cunnian   —'

The tongue.

Oozing out. Once again.

Extrudes, without pause. Its gelatinous tip snakes between the futons. And stops. And coils itself around the waist of a stocky young woman in a black and violet smock. Seated at the front. Hoists her up. Waves her about in the air. Gurgles in celebration. Retracts.

Swallows her.

Whole.

The light. Such as it is. Dims even further.

The giant worm slithers back to its lair.

The green rocks and red trees

deconstruct themselves.

Seep into

noir.

The screen changes:

```
::: ::: LES FUTONS INFERNAUX ::: :::

: 18 :

' LA DANSE '
```

Music.
Mellow pipes.
Joined by the *throb throb,*
throb throb, of a drum machine.

The entire
petrology of sound
segues into disco. Softens.

A tenor larynx launches
into howls of psychic lechery
overlaid with a sweetly muted horn.
The rhythm dips. The lights come back on.

A distant acre away
he catches spasmodic sightings
of a tiny dancing figure.

Moving from side to side
but mostly lost behind what he conjectures are the dim silhouettes of rocks and tree trunks. Dancing. Corybantic. From tree to tree. From rock to rock. Drawing closer. Coming into focus. A young woman. Smocked in black and violet. The spotlight pursues her, fitfully catching fire in the coloured tassels of her dreadlocked hair, bunched at the top and flanking her heart-shaped face with vertical cascades of green and purple.

The rhythm insists.
Grips him. By the belly, the groin, the marrow.
He finds himself swaying and foot-tapping on his futon. Stands. Scuttling. Forwards. Backwards. Sideways. Gyrating. Swinging his hips. Pointing and punching out the air. He glances at the audience through the gloom, puzzled that no-one else has been moved to join in.

Each foot, nailed to the floor.
Each bottom, welded
to its leather seat.

Young and old.
Male and female.

All aloof. He doesn't get it.

The girl with the braids is moving ever closer, navigating through the plywood trees and cardboard rocks. Short and squat and vital, with a squareness about her that blocks neither the energy nor fluidity of her dance.

She is performing for him, him alone.

Framed in green and purple, her face looks unremarkable. But disarmingly friendly. Familiar, but in some way he doesn't understand. They are together now and dancing in a weird communion like nothing he has known before. 'You're a lovely dancer,' she exclaims. Their limbs twisting and stomping in ecstatic collusion.

She vanishes.

And just as suddenly

reappears holding two glasses of wine.

Sitting down on his futon she motions him to join her. Which he does. They drink. He starts to chat. She takes both his hands and kisses him on the lips. He understands now why her face seems so familiar.

He is looking at himself.

They stand.

And dance again.

She grows ever more extraordinary.

Back on his futon,
they cling together.

And start weeping,
as the two halves
of the futon
separate.

Drowning.
In dust.
In must.
In horsehair.

Sucked.
Subsumed.
Ingested, by
its inner core
- — -

Regaining
consciousness.
He is alone on his futon.

No sign of the girl.
The same people. Less one of course.
On the same futons. The same silence.

Holds his head. In his hands.

Wondering.

What next ?

A tap-tapping.
A murmuring. In the audience.
Onto centre-stage falters an aged gentilhomme with long
white hair and a long white staff. Enrobed as Archimandrite.
In a vair-trimmed soutane of purple silk.
Tap-tapping. Blind.

The empty albinic eyes
stare up at the screen:

```
::: ::: LES FUTONS INFERNAUX ::: :::

: 19 :

' LE CHEVALIER '
```

The thin albinic mouth
opens to speak.
Orates…

Once.

Once. Once.

Long ago in a land limned by lovelessness a tale there was told of a certain Knight, a great City and a sacred Grail. The Knight was brave and the City wondrous beyond all imagining. The Grail however, existed only as a glittering fantasy alchemised from the fear and solitude of the land's illiterate serfdom and its inbred imbecilic aristocracy.

Notwithstanding this,
the quest for the Grail was the Knight's mission.
And so it was that this singularly quixotic paragon strode out onto the pulpwood proscenia of his birthland and spoke words of such eloquence that serfs and nobles alike were persuaded that his cause was both necessary and achievable. In consequence he was presented by the ruling oligarchs with a retinue of armed assistants, a battalion of horse-drawn bazookas and a copious expenses fund.

Because his given name was unpronounceable and his facial features tended to transmogrify every thirty-five minutes, the Knight wore a flesh-tinted rubber mask fashioned into a likeness of that future wartime film-actor and toothy singing comedian, Sir George Formby. He was known to all, throughout the land, as Sir George.

The legend of Sir George, his covenanted followers and their pitiable hunt for that elusive Grail was lost for many generations until the dawn of last year's summer solstice, when it fell out of a generic corn flakes packet as a plastic toy submarine of a mere two inches in length. When the young boy who found it placed the submarine in hot bathwater a tendril of oily black smoke squirmed from its conning tower, snaked its way to the nearest wall and began writing in a compact ancient calligraphy.

The writing continued until every wall of the child's house was covered. It foretold the numerous disappearances and rediscoveries of the great legend and described how Sir George, his armoury and his retinue would travel through many perilous lands and landscapes in ever-hopeful confusion before arriving, by means of a labyrinthine underground stone quarry, at the unique and much-fabled City of Rictus Aeternus.

The quarry itself was a maze of abandoned limestone and granite mines dating from the Roman epoch. Many were the months spent by Sir George and his men in their desperate search for a way through these ancient tunnels to the legendary City. The round-arched, massively pillared limestone workings of the Romans, allied with the square and more practical arches of the Saxons and Normans, yielded a prodigious complex of caverns and galleries.

As Sir George and his retinue navigated by sputtering tallow and debilitated instinct through these mephistophelean chambers, they scratched crude epigrams of humour and despair into the comminuted shells of the huge pillars. On one of these, inscribed centuries before, was a tale Sir George would never forget.

The tale of Newton Poppleford, a stone-carter from the nearby village of Fingest. To augment the meagre repasts of his starving family this hapless carter would use his lead-tipped horsewhip to lasso muscovy ducks from a pond outside the Manor House. He was eventually caught by the Lord of the Manor, tried by this same Lord and transported to the hinterlands of Australia, where he languished and died, so they say, of a broken heart.

After four months of freezing frustration, just as provisions were running out, with half his retinue dead from malnutrition or hyperthermia, with all of his horses killed for meat and his bazookas abandoned, Sir George happened upon the intricately carved oak door of the City. He and his men put their emaciated shoulders to the door's magnificent edge and were amazed when it creaked slowly open.

Before them arose a wall of smooth black onyx. Infinitely high. Infinitely wide. Bolted close to it was a narrow ladder extending some fifty metres up the wall to a small aperture through which seeped a thin amber light. The ladder seemed ramshackle, and appeared to have been assembled from lashed-together, gold-painted, human leg bones.

Strapping his gear to his back, Sir George began the climb, followed at some distance by his remaining attendants. The ladder was damp and slippery, becoming more so the higher the men climbed. In addition the rungs cracked alarmingly as soon as any weight was applied.

At regular intervals a scream would echo round the darkness signifying another follower had fallen to his death on the rock floor. Nonetheless the Knight forced himself higher until he came to the top rung, where he was able to rest his elbows at last on the sill of a rough-hewn window.

What he saw astonished him.
Below, above and beyond lay the interior of an enormous, cathedral-like barn, strewn with knolls of straw bales, broken open and falling apart from their binding twine.

Straw was everywhere.
Most especially beneath his forearms. Stabbing his flesh. Covering everything. Ignited to a honeyed patchwork by the sunlight streaming in through the leaded windows, it was further refracted by a kaleidoscope of brightly coloured, blown-glass panes.

Abutting the oblong of his primitive window, the bales were stacked high enough to be flush with the sill, allowing an easy exit onto the plateau of coarse stubble.

As the first of his men, a big-boned young chef called Flute, was hauling himself through the window, there came a sudden crunching noise followed by an eruption of yells.

The ladder was breaking up.

Sir George scrambled back to help the youth, whose feet were kicking air. He grabbed him by the wrists. But they were too greasy. The grip slipped to hooked fingers, which held better. With their fingers clamped together the Knight threw all his remaining strength into winching the exhausted boy up over the edge.

But the effort was too much.

Flute's grip weakened. Sir George moaned in anguish as the lax fingers slithered through his own and the plucky young chef fell uncomplaining to his death.

The bereft and barely conscious Knight crawled back from the sill, buried his face in the straw, and wept an unobserved, heartfelt tear into his George Formby mask.

Sitting up to swallow the last dirty drop from his water bottle, he was struck, even in his current state of atrophy and fatigue, by the golden, revelatory glare of the light.

Lying down in shock,
he drifted into
a deep sleep.

And woke.
Much later.

And stood.
Momentarily blinded
by a harsh glister in the air.

*   *   *

Something is different.

The straw-packed barn
is just as he remembers.
But something is different.

It comes to him as vatic epiphany.
Everything. Everywhere. Immersed in brilliance. Encased in a solid and stainless bubble. An intense panoptic jewel that the

midday sun has struck. Into itself this celestial gem has received him, just as springwater accepts a fresh ray of light while remaining intact and inviolate.

All around him syntheses of flame fly upward from the baled and unbaled clusters of straw. To astral frequencies of music and reverberant canticles of desire, their fusions of energy converge into a single vague and limitless form
of the brightest
palest fire.

He cannot but
gaze into its empty centre.
To turn away would be fatal.

In its measureless depth
he sees gathered and bound by love
into one sacred tome what in the universe seems separate and scattered. Substances, accidents and dispositions as if conjoined. A universal shape. A lustrous core containing everything that has been and everything that can be, containing all places and all actions, seen from all angles and at every instant of their existence and process.

The Grail is his.
His alone.

Sir George has gained at last the object of his quest and insomuch
as he can keep all of his intellect, all of his senses
and all of his innermost self
focussed on its boundless
hubless coruscation
he will know
himself
forever

as

Y e H o V a H

*   *   *

The
blind storyteller
shuffles out of the light.

Tap-tap.

Tap-tap.

Tap-tap.

5. Schutz

Schutz

48

One

hour or

one day later,

with zilch in his wallet,
and the freebio plonko rosso
still rampaging through his blood,
he falls or is pushed out of a filthy old Fiat
onto the fractious yellow tarmac
of Tufnell Park Road.

Rain.
Still pissing down, dropping
in erratic windshook tankfuls
from the canopy of plane trees.

Over the kerb he limps.
Through the gelid swamp of the grass verge. Onto the wet
pavement. The Elisabeth Street mansions look as angry,
monstrous and miserable as ever.

Drunk as a slug and still bombed by greasy rainballs from the
overhead flumes of bark and bone, he stumbles and squirms
his way up the giant Victorian steps
of his landlady's
castle.

5am.

Mrs Schrödinger's front parlour.

Asleep.

Laid flat back on the Schrödinger double sofa before a dyspeptic three-bar electric fire with her dead husband's dressing gown veneered to his skin, he wakes to find himself suffocating under some thick material which he soon identifies as warm garlic widow-breath freighted to him by the words of the said widow as she relates yet again the saga of her beloved late spouse's failed attempt on the life of the Yorkshire Ripper as the disgraced former art connoisseur did his weekly rounds delivering laundry to the wards

of Broadmoor Prison Hospital.

Yet again she is complaining how troublesome life is for the grieving widow of a German national while Q is reflecting on how troublesome life is for a half-dead young artist who only wants to sleep or puke but is being kept awake by a brown scaly hand on his thigh which every twenty to thirty seconds digs a sharp blood-red nail into the skin between his kneecap and his tibial biceps tendon.

And all this while.

The agricultural breath crawls all over him.

The ways to be free seem ever more obstructed.

So stuck is he in the knot
of his and other people's
fantasies.

The simple teenage grub
in his almost adult heart.
Spills spunk,
glair.

He knows this is what he wants.
What he needs. Knows it well.
But the widow's putrid breath.
The rasping piston
of her voice.

And now.
Her other hand.
On his gut.

The hand on his thigh is hot and painful. On his belly, its
circumambulatory twin is ponderous, blind and persistent.
She whispers that her fingers are simply demonstrating a
range of therapeutic procedures from the zen massage canon.
The voice purrs on and on. Relentless. But. The enigma of her
housecoated woman's body intrigues him.
He wants it. Wants.

No. No-no.

He leans forward.

Crushes the resolute fingers.

Pushes himself up with a mumbled excuse
and drags his dead limbs upstairs
to his attic flat.

Seated at last
on the edge of his bed,
he opens his sodden manbag, relieved to find the small
sketchbook still dry in its polythene sleeve. His clothes are
still drip-drip-dripping on an old wooden frame next to the
radiator where Mrs Schrödinger hung them an hour ago.

A 60 watt bulb dangles by a furry ten-foot flex from its snot-
washed ceiling rose, throwing a soft but adequate light on the
adjacent studio easel.

He retrieves
a large sketchbook
from his bedside chest.
Turns to a fresh page. From a grape-size glob of Indian ink
expressed from an antediluvian fountain pen he spreads lines
and blots and smudges across the heavy paper.
Spits on it.

Scratches into it. Tears into it. Attempts to replicate the dense
energy of the bald stripper's presence and pose.

Not unhappy, he downs the pen.
Wipes his hands on the lumpy counterpane.

Closes his eyes…
                        and summons
the idea of Miriam X
into his room.

With her back to him
she shrugs a blue poncho from her shoulders.

Twists around.
Grins.

Strides
towards him.
And through him.
As if he were nothing.

He curses.
Falls back on his pillow.
Topples into…
                        a troubled sleep.

Eugène.
Materialises.
Contemplates the sleeper.
Looks with unease
at the drawing.

Sits on the bed,
takes Q's hand
in his own.

Starts humming,

    'It's A Dream',
        a tender, not
            unsentimental

                ditty,
      from
            the back catalogue
            of

                Neil Young

6.   **Three Scabs**

Three Scabs

s.1

that sun
that August

that
afternoon

that bike
and those wheels those
wheels on the bike wheels
on the bike wheels on the
bike wheels on the bike
wheels on the bike and
that wind the warm
wind in his face
midges in the
wind flying
ants in his
hair eyes
mouth.

Bent low
on his father's
demotorised BSA racing bike.
Drop handlebars. Sticky green tape for grips.

Leaving the village behind, he plunges into grassfields and cornfields. On a carless road. The Branwell Baldwin cricket pavilion slips by to his left. And then barns and farms, and cows and pigs and more cows and still the rackety rusty wheels of his father's bike. Up slopes and down slopes. And still no cars and still the warm wind and the ants in his face and the same dense cloud of midges for implacable escort. Navigates around potholes. Crevasses. Mangled pheasants.

A five mile ride. Thighs already aching.

He's never liked bikes.

But come what may.

He's on his way.

His eighteen-year-old date lives in a prefab bungalow on the American air base. With her parents. But alone now.

Waiting. Expecting him. Miriam X. Alone. Waiting.

Short. Sharp. Sad. A slender fox cub presence.

Small-breasted body. Curly, too-greasy hair.

Pugnacious. Coquettish. Moral.

'Christ, you're a mess,' she grins. Pulls him inside.

Hands him a glass of home-brewed cider.

Which he guzzles down.

She offers a walk.

He agrees.

Out of the air base they maunder. Through the hamlet and
onto a public footpath secreted in a gap between two walled
gardens. The path is gravelled and narrow with fierce nettles
leaning in from both sides. Forcing them close.
Their bare arms bump and graze.

They emerge smiling and unstung into a wildflower
meadow. A few jersey cows in the distance.
Along a worn path. At the field's rim.
By a bramble hedge.

And arrive.
At an unkempt pond.
Ringed by ash and pussy willow.
On either side, a cornfield.
One of wheat.
One of barley.

The hedge is disrupted
by a broken stile.

They chomp and chew
on rubbery grains of wheat.
Clamber over the stile. Play
stupid laughing darts
with the barley.

She sits on the stile. Pulls him to her.
Her kisses are soft. Sapient. Slow.
Her hand drops. To his groin.
Fervour falters.

He blurts *not now* as her fingers slip inside his fly.
Lowering her sandaled feet to the grass,
she giggles and leads him in a daze
back to the bungalow.

'They're out for the day,' she whispers,
drawing him into her yellow bedroom
onto her yellow bed.
Both yellow naked
under the sheets.

Is it the factory tang of the condom ?
Her totally breastless body ?
Too much anticipation ?
Whatever.

She's kind. But.
Washing up crockery.
Afterwards. In the kitchen.
With her back to him. She sings along to the radio.
'… *gonna wash that man right outa* …'

So that,

he determines

on the windblown

bike-ride home,

is that

…

if
only

*   *   *

Q
snorts.
Bares his teeth.
Turns to lie on his other shoulder.

Eugène smiles.
Leans forward.
Kisses his young friend.
On the temple.

s.2

that sun
that August

that

afternoon

Chris ?

Christopher ?

Is that you ?
First friend, dissentient runt, in exile
from the harsh benevolence of your ma and pa,
the world's completest foreigner,
your very flesh in red revolt
against its hectic blood.

Was it you at his side on Ipston Common,
idling out that dog-hot summer's pocketmoney day ?

Do you remember, remember, remember
that day you burned down Buckinghamshire ?

Do you remember how you crouched beside
that screwed-up heap of yellow tubes and paper ?

Do you remember how your tongue was
thick with sherbet froth and liquorice ?

Do you remember how the rattle of the matches
in their wood and cardboard box was apotheotic drum-roll
to your ten-year power-hungry hearts ?

Were you with him when he lit the dusty grass and gorse
with that single dynamite swan vesta ?

Were you with him in the blueing
of the flame ?

Were you with him
in the eggy glare of early afternoon
as fear leapt in giant leapings with the fire ?

Do you remember how you stamped and spun ?

How the knee-high heat caught and crackled open
that first dry drift of gorse ?

How the many
in that clump of prickled dark deniers
joined in to spit and roar
their disapproval ?

Did you
gallop with him
from that theatre of flame,
over the Ipston cricket pitch,
over the uncut common,
over the empty road,
to home ?

Were you
standing with him
at his attic window ?

Did
you hear
the engine of
the big red ruckus
you'd concocted ?

Did
you see
the village devils
in their doorways ?
mouthing ? bunching ?
plotting ?

What happened ?

What happened to the bruised laughter ?
The cuts ? The brilliantine ?

What happened, that day you vanished
with the smoke and steam ?

Christopher ?

Chris ?

*   *   *

Eugène
permits his
decrepit old goatee
an affectionate stroke.

Gives his bony old shoulder
a gentle squeeze.

Sighs. Slowly
rotates his
head.

s.3

that sun
that August

that

afternoon

that phone call,
that same old journey.

And Jessica. His mother.
Swollen-eyed. At her front door.
In a wildly inappropriate summer dress.
Flecked with scarlet pansies.
Mauve butterflies.
Telling him.

How Garth, his father, walked out. Suddenly.
A week ago. Gone midnight. No warning.
Left everything. Even his Bentley.
Without a word.
Nothing.

Q stays over.
A long, long weekend.

Her twin arrives.
Aunt Madge. To help out.
He leaves on Tuesday.

Taxi to Stornchurch.
Bus to High Wycombe.
An endless, upstairs, front-seat crawl, with
Mrs Robertson-Ortiz sweating at his side,
meaning well but clueless at consolation.
And himself numb, bereft of a father
he'd never even started
to understand
or like.

Cernuous branches
of beech and oak and sycamore
crash up against the windows in dismay.
And all the while the breathy words of his mother's
man-eating neighbour are wooing him deeper into decline.
Cadmium orange wheatfields flash past,
strobing the woody glades.

He sleeps on the train.
Wycombe to Kings Cross.
Accomplishes with mortified relief
the stifling subterranean trek to his Tufnell Park flat.

Drags off his clothes. Rolls onto the unmade bed.

Plummets into pain.

Treacle. Heat.

*

Dawn. A few days later.

Woken by the usual radio babble

from the flat next door.

Teeth.

Shave. Shower.

Coffee and croissant. Phone Jessica.

'I'm okay, love. Madge's still here, but the Bentley's gone.

Someone's broken into the garage and driven it off.

The police will be here soon.'

Two hours pass. A phone call.

'They've just left. The studio was burnt down. Last night.

Arson, they said. Nothing makes sense.

I just don't understand.

What's happening?'

Two weeks pass. Another phone call. Early evening.

He doesn't recognise the pinched voice.

'Hello dear. It's Aunt Madge.'

'Auntie… ?'

In tears.
She tells him.
His mother died an hour ago.
Found unconscious in the morning.
Rushed by ambulance to Wycombe Hospital.
Stomach pumped, but no use.
Heart pills, they said.

Suicide ?

'That's how it looks.
She was so down and confused.
And so lost. I did my best. I'm sorry, sweetheart.'
Hammering it home…

'The final straw was the gossip,
a shedload of hearsay and tittletattle
about your dad and a couple of village girls,
behind the pub toilets, then back to his studio.'

A not infrequent event,
according to rumour.

'The truth hit poor Jessie like a bombshell.
She knew nothing about it, any more than I did.
What a sly deceitful wretch. All that time.
I'm sorry dear, but good riddance.
Wherever he is…'

Hell.

Hell.

Hell.

*   *   *

The bicentenarian painter
stretches. Yawns.
Rubs his eyes.

Lays a bygone bony hand
on the sleeper's brow.

Flickers. Fades.

Walks out

7.   Genitor

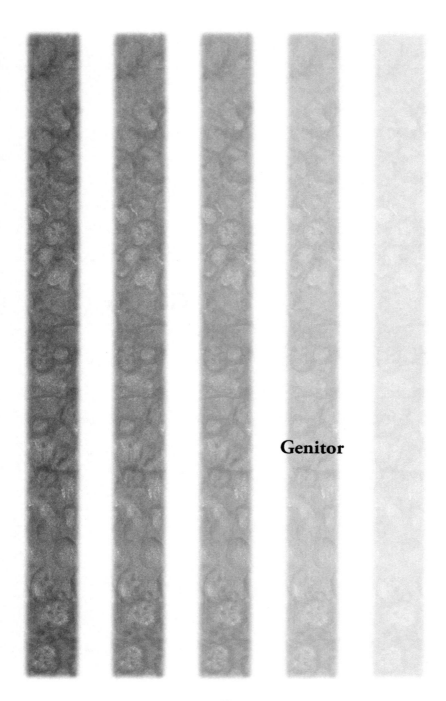

Genitor

72

A short man.

Shorter than his son.

Shorter than his wife.

He of the corrugate cupola.

Side-parted and swept left in a five-inch, raw sienna tsunami. The spine, stiff and straight. The baked-potato head, held ever high and back. The eyes, cold and colourless, inflated to lagoons of liquid anonymity by his cerulean-framed, myopically thick, non-prescription spectacles.

Up until his abrupt exit he was Head of Art at Wycombe Academy, a fee-charging co-ed anachronism kept alive by the shabbiness of the local alternatives. The young students were all held willy-nilly in line by his air of profound inviolability and overweening self-absorption. Executing his rounds during sixth form art lessons, pointing to this girl's careless error and that boy's risible misprision, there was a certain something in his aura. An edge. A threat. A feeling that if confronted he could and indeed would inflict severe psychological damage on the upstart challenger to his judgement and authority.

When performing his showy doggerel poetry however, he became to his pupils curiously human and even likable, expressing in rumty-tum rhythm and with tetchy wit a repugnance for the tedium of provincial life and a contempt for their prudish fellow-townsfolk. A frequent invitee at

South Buckinghamshire poetry gatherings, he could always be counted on to attract half a dozen disgruntled adolescents, thereby expanding considerably the otherwise sparse and elderly demographic.

Bit of a rebel.

After all.

Non-school days were spent either socialising in pubs or working in his studio. It was here, in a brick-and-timber stable-conversion leased from an Ipston farmer, that he produced his weirdly saleable pieces of artwork. The paintings were cartoonoid faux-naïf. Erotically prinked. Archly semi-offensive. All of which bolstered his reputation as local offbeat anti-hero, but without the need of his offering any real ammunition to undermine the timid conventions which he affected to despise, and without of course ever risking his social and financial security.

Time at home with his wife and son was reduced over the years to a bare and fickle minimum. The mood of distracted indifference never left him. Even here.

Despite frequent goading by his teenage son, he would invariably decline to be drawn into serious discussion about Art or Poetry or Music. Q could never understand this and began eventually to attribute his father's evasiveness to a fear that his intricately groomed persona might be exposed through scrutiny as a gutless fraud. The slightest attempt by his son to engage in non-trivial debate around their supposedly shared interests would be met with the same old grunts, and the same old bluster.

*　*　*

Early evening. Q's bedroom.
His seventeenth birthday.
The door opens.

'Happy birthday, Quasimodo. No revision?'

'Thanks. All done.'

'What you reading?'

'Gertrude Stein.'

'Aaaah. Okay.'

The door shuts.

Q hollers through it, 'I'm going to Art School!'

The door re-opens.

'Fine. Tell your mother. She won't be pleased.'

The door re-shuts.

A rattle of keys.
A glissando of footsteps
Along the garden path. Out the gate.
Onto gravel.

The garage rollers grind up.

A car door opens.

The Bentley coughs out a rat
from its gut,

                         sputters,

             revs,

         rumbles backward.
Stops.

The rollers grind down.

Car wheels crunch…

move off…

8. Hell Cottage

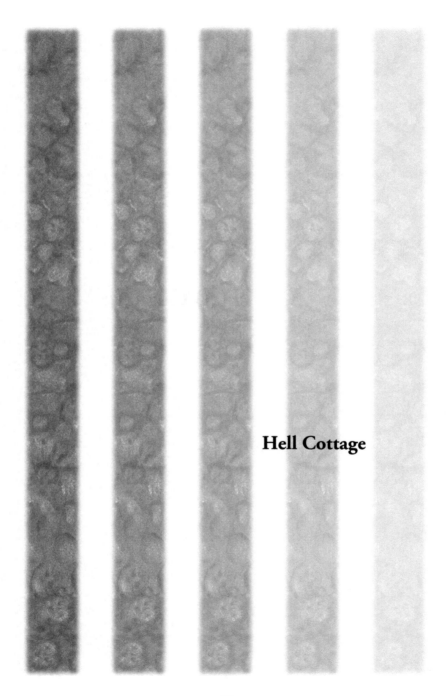

Hell Cottage

Ipston.

Mid-September.

A year since the suicide.

The tyro.

On his way to Hell Corner.

To visit Belinda Manningtree.

A former nurse and friend of his father, she'd once posed scandalously nude for an extended series of comic-strippy Chaucerian mise-en-scènes painted in sub-pedo-Schiele mode. Garth's most popular work.

As it turned out.

After the bus from Wycombe and a hot sunny trek from Stornchurch he cuts across the village Common, striding sacrilegiously over the shaved cricket square. Through the outfield stubble. Through his old adversary the gorse patch. Onto the tree-shadowed tarmac of Cripplegate Lane.

Floats past the pavilion.

Eddies with murderous emotion

past the charred wreck of his father's studio,

set back from the road but barely visible now

behind its fence of convolvulus-clogged chickenwire.

He slows down.

Where the Lane terminates he's no idea.

He and his pal Christopher never ventured beyond Hell Corner Farm, and seldom beyond Hell Wood, which still holds the alluring strangeness of Belinda the Wood Witch, and of Hell Cottage, her notorious sanctum sanctorum.

By itself in a beech-girt glade directly south of the Lane, her modest one storey cottage stands on the site of an inglorious public execution, a grisly auto-da-fé conducted in the 1640s at the height of the Protestant witch-hunt epidemic by one Jacob Stearne, an acquaintance and evangelical ally of the self-styled Witchfinder General himself.

Although its foundations were dug in the mid-1750s, the bungalow took over eighty years to complete. As soon as the brickwork reached twelve courses high or more, it was, according to the legend, demolished back to rubble in the dead of night by Satan and his Demons, in payback for the immolation of his favourite Priestess. Many attempts were made. Always with the same result. The fame of the enterprise spread until eventually the outer shell of the cottage was constructed in a single day by a team of twenty bricklayers and then frantically exorcised before nightfall by the Bishop of Oxford. The whole area has been known as Hell Corner ever since, despite the fact that no further supernatural incidents were ever recorded.

His boots.

Are noiseless.

On the tarred grit.

Birdsong. Birdrustle.

From the woods to his left and the hedgerow to his right. These are the only sounds ruffling the alien tranquillity of this close and windless afternoon, the only sounds to merge in placid rapport with the tidal drift of his breathing.

Trudging down the gentle incline, he finds himself at long last near a familiar, fondly remembered hiatus in the tall bracken ramparts encompassing the wooded vale.

Off the tarmac, onto the grass verge.

A plush fertile mattress.

And into the wood.

Hell Wood.

Sudden. Cool.

Resonant with its own sharded dramas of light and dark. Staved by the fresh and the dead trunks of beech and oak and the occasional sycamore. He discovers once again the scooped-out bomb-site boulevard which used to take him and his young friend down through the shallow escarpment to their destination. All around lie the limbs and torsos of a wind-felled army. A warzone of uprooted trees. He clambers

over the trunk of a gargantuan beech, mouldering to a deep
Indian red on its blazing stage.
The New. Still fighting the Old.
Life against Death.

Everywhere spattered
in guerrilla greens. Of emerald. Olive. Viridian.
A rescue-poultice of mosses and ferns administered in
tessellated blotches to the dermis of geriatric decay. And
oilblack holly, growing in the most unimaginable places,
sprouting parasitically from the ankles of adolescent beeches,
clawing its way to incredible heights, but always as the
uninvited tenant of its more massive fellows.

And underfoot. A fritillaried sackcloth of dead leaves. Dead
twigs. Dead beechmast. But all crunching so sweetly beneath
his boots that it seems he himself is being savoured, chewed
and devoured by the rebirthing senescence of some enchanted,
Gaian Ur-Forest.

As ever,
he comes to it unexpectedly.
Seen from above, its umber roof is refracted by the light into a
gauze of fine-woven kestrel feathers. But despite this. Despite
the affable sun. Despite the lovingly nurtured roses in the
front garden. Despite the wisteria-decked porch.
This is no fairytale cottage.

Ninety years ago it was seared and blackened by a woodland fire and has never lost its gangrenous scowl. The uninsured bungalow was gutted by the flames, sold off cheap and renovated to a very low standard. Electricity from the National Grid was installed but the water is still hand-pumped into the roof tank from an underground stream first discovered and used shortly after the Restoration. Its only toilet is still not much more than an outhouse latrine.

He pushes open the ramshackle gate.
Walks onto the brick path.

He knows Belinda from the days of his scary games with Christopher. Playing up to her sinister reputation, she would tease and jest and prank with them but always invite them in afterwards for apple juice and hobnobs. He recalls though that it was never for more than half an hour and the excuse for getting rid of them was never the same.

With a smile on his face, he approaches the jaded melamine of the front door, listening out for her shrill, little-girl voice, normally in animated conversation with her tomcat, in those days a playful tabby, but now, so he's heard,
a stand-offish maine coon.

He presses the bell.

Somewhat surprisingly
it actually works and triggers
an echoey peal of ecclesiastical chimes.

'Oh. It's you, dear. Goodness. Do come in.'

The woman before him is so small, so slight, and her voice
so querulous that he wonders should he have come. But the
smile is genuine and the workworn fingers are tight on his
arms as she hugs him to her. As always, the make-up is too
heavy, almost but not quite at odds with her fragile features.
The mouth is thin-lipped and sensitive, deeply creased in one
corner. The nose is stubbornly plebeian but the grey eyes glint
like quicksilver. The hair is thick and wavy, neatly bobbed
and tinted to a musty blonde.
She leads him to the double sofa.
Pulls him down. Beside her.
He looks round.

The small living room is shoddily decorated in off-white
emulsion, applied in thick uneven brushstrokes and blotched
by damp and wear. Four of his father's paintings are hung,
skew-whiff, on the walls. Early episodes from the punk-
Chaucerian series.

The maine coon appears from nowhere. Rubs its grey skull
against his shin. 'This is Marcus Aurelius,' she chuckles. 'Your

dad called him that. Good boy, Marcus.' The lynx-like beast disappears under the sofa as she starts to recount something of her on-off affair with Garth. How she felt more and more exploited until finally she said 'enough'. How they stayed kind-of friends. How she would still pose for him occasionally, right up to the end.

'I know you were angry when you came here four years ago. I don't blame you, although the relationship itself was over by then. But you shouldn't have been so nasty to Jasmine. I suppose it just boiled over.' She offers him tea. He declines. She continues. 'I feel bad about your mother though. To think she was completely in the dark all those years. Garth said she knew and was okay with it, and I believed him because it suited me I guess. But I soon learned never to take anything he said at face value. Such a fool I was. But you know I can't honestly regret it because we did have some happy times and those paintings he made of me did gave him his little bit of local success.'

She blushes.
He asks about his father's disappearance.
'He came straight here that night but wouldn't tell me anything. Stayed all next day until nightfall, when three brutish-looking men came for him. He left with them. Seemed worried all the time. But thoughtful, considerate. At least for him. And didn't mind sleeping on the sofa thank

goodness. That was the last time I saw him. Those men were horrible. He seemed down and defeated in some way.
I knew he wouldn't be back.'

A tap squeaks.
'Jaz,' Belinda calls out.
Nineteen-year-old Jasmine enters the room. Stands in the kitchen doorway. Head down. Short. Sullen-shouldered.
Her long black tresses hiding all thought and emotion.

'Hullo Q,' she murmurs.

'She's doing an Art History degree. At the Courtauld Institute, starting next week. Aren't you dear?'

Q is intrigued.
Pushes himself up, with relief,
from the grievously unaccommodating sofa.

'That sounds great' he says. 'I love the Courtauld. Let's meet up for a chat sometime when you're in London. Perhaps one day after I've finished work at the Schools. They don't mind me doing that, popping in sometimes to draw or paint from the model, although I've got my degree and officially left. The Keeper's a sweet guy and seems to like me for some strange reason. Can I call you?'

She lifts her head, parting as she does so the dark swags of her hair. 'Okay. That might be nice.'

They swap phone numbers. She has changed a lot in four years. For him, the memory is a guilty and unpleasant one. Her black eyes seem bigger now. More haunted. Her features fuller. Stronger. Pugnacious even.

Turning back to the kitchen,
she flashes him a grin.

He decides he likes her.
'Sorry I was rude to you back then,' he calls out.

'Don't worry. It was ages ago,' floats back the reply.

Ready to leave,
he shoulders his bag.

Belinda takes his arm as he walks to the door.
'I almost forgot,' she says. 'Funny you dropping by today. Who d'you think called in only last week?'

'Not Christopher, surely?'

'I couldn't believe it. He seemed okay, too. Works as a warden for the Forestry Commission And really enjoys it. He came to the village to see his mother, who's not in good health. His father died ten years ago and I don't think she misses him to be honest. She's always kind to me when we meet in the village shop, unlike a lot of people round here. And she's still living in the old School House, which they bought when the school itself moved to Stornchurch. A good headmistress she was, and the kids liked her, even though she was strict. But her architect husband was a cold unpleasant man, which didn't sit well with them being Quakers I always thought. Young Christopher was a big disappointment to him so I gather, and just because the lad wasn't academic like himself. They paid for him to attend Magdalen College School but soon took him out because of the bullying. Sent him eventually to a progressive private school in the New Forest where he was much happier, or so the lad told me. At least it took him away from his moaning father. Oh, and his eczema is all cleared up. He's still shy. But he came. And I was so pleased to see him!'

'That's wonderful to hear. We didn't have much in common except being teachers' sons. But we were lonely and good for each other. Together against the world and all that stuff. Anyway it's getting dark now, so…
Goodnight, Belinda.'

Back in the woods,
on his way to The Rabbit, Ipston's one and only pub,

where he is booked in for the night, he tries to plan ahead.
Kicks impatiently at the dead leaves and beech debris.
Marooned holly berries gleam their acute redness,
their spiky violence, directly up at him
through the dusk.

He had forgotten
the dumb, stupid fears.
The loneliness. Of a country night.

Relieved as he might be to leave behind the whispers of the
hostile trees and sense the firm hard tarmac under his feet,
Cripplegate Lane after dark still feels just as closed-in and
threatening as ever.

The tedious stretch of main road leading uphill from
Cripplegate Lane to The Rabbit has tripled in length.
Solely for his benefit.

He pushes open the door to the Saloon.
Even without its rhino-boned, gorilla-skinned, fag-smoking
farmworkers of dim and detestable memory, the pub's interior
is just as acrid, just as wreathed in toxic miasmas as it was in
the nights of his youth. He sits.
Peruses the menu.
Orders.

Memories notwithstanding,
the dinner proves adequate and
the wine most welcome.

But he is glad
to pull the clean bedsheet
up to his chin. And drift.
Finally. Into sleep.

Could it?
Could it really have been?

In the Bentley? In the Soho snow?
Last April?

                                      *   *   *

                              Eugène says nothing.

                                 He too is sleeping.

                                    Eyes closed.

9.   The Schools

The Schools

Up.

Up out of.

The blighted borehole.

Auto-zigzagging an eastward itinerary.

Through and between the Piccadilly wage slaves.

10am. The tyro swings north and grits his beaver teeth together through the spangled elongated crypt of Burlington Arcade. Then east and sharp south into the cobbled, walled-in back passage of his Alma Mater. The pomposity of its Palladian fabric has always seemed to him both farcically at odds and farcically in keeping with the vapid squalor of most of the crimes committed within its walls.

The door marked 'STUDENTS' is open.

The Royal Academy Schools. He steps over the timeworn threshold. Nods to Jeremiah Gilpin, the swarthily mildewed red-and-black-liveried Head Porter-cum-Gatekeeper. Signs the register in the bleak office. 'Morning, Jerry,' he chirrups. Gilpin, who hates students, glares back at him.

The twilight of the entrance lobby is overlorded by a glossy black cast of *Laocoön and his Sons*. A rather witty placement in Q's opinion, although whom is being referenced by sea serpents, warrior priest and his two diminutive sons changes capriciously every time he sees it.

Throwing over his shoulder the faux-leather hold-all containing his painting gear and his book of Michelangelo sonnets, he descends the spiral staircase.

Along the 150-year-old mall.
Clichéd flaky icons of carved-and-cast
mockmarble antiquity snigger down at him
from their elevated plinths. Dusty chandeliers
light his way to the Life Painting Studio.
But the flagstone floor. Is clean.
Hard. True.

Inside. All is as it should be.
Eve, the emaciated model, is sitting on her cushioned high-backed barstool. She looks thinner every week. To his surprise, among the usual barricaded domains of the usual busy students stands Izzy Higgs. At an easel. Lost in thought. Or something else not very similar. But drawing. Clutched in his hands is an egg-shaped chunk of charcoal. And a big black rubber. Spraying his usual sooty blizzard onto the polished parquet tiles.

Q catches his eye. Grins.
Finds and pulls out his own well-worked-on canvas from the long wall rack. In the space allotted to him he sets up calmly. Easel. Palette table. Tins and tubes.
Budget oil paint.

In ten minutes he is up and running and appalled by the ineptness of last week's marks and daubs. Nothing whatsoever to do with the explosive presence before him. The seated model. Scrape off. Start. Start again. With broad arcs of sludge and line. Until something of the tension, the balance, the vitality of the model's pose sneaks through the cobwebby bastions of custom and praxis.

Anxiety
of influence
is another test.
How to rid one's brush…
one's palette… one's head…
of… Titian. Hopper. Bacon.
Cezanne. Giacometti. Soutine…
All those glorious, devious, deadly heroes.

Simple.
Immersion.
Utter immersion.
The answer to everything.
And then the model breaks.
Everyone breaks.
For coffee.

He sighs. Downs rag and brushes.
Ambles over to Izzy.

They stroll to the canteen.

'Didn't expect to see you here,' remarks Q over their double espressos. 'Likewise,' responds Izzy, emptying three sachets of demerara into his cup. 'Been here a couple of times recently. When work stuff gets me down. The shop's doing okayish but it's always hand to mouth and the drawing relaxes me. And it's free. And to be honest I really enjoy it. Though the struggling artist palaver never grabbed me by the bollocks like it did you. Anyway. You doing alright?'

'Fine thanks. Came into a spot of money when my mum died, so… well… At least it means I don't have to work the building sites any more. Just the occasional couple of days decorating when I need to.'

'Selling much?'

'You know me, Izz. Never was going to be flavour of the month. Unlike Koki over there.' They glance across the tables at a shabby-chic young dude with tinted shades entertaining with artful ease a bevy of student admirers.

'Good luck to him though. Seems a decent enough guy. But in spite of everything I'm working pretty hard and it feels like I might be getting somewhere at last.
But who knows…?'

'Yeah. You always were an awkward bugger. Don't forget you're welcome to hang a few in the gallery bit of my shop. Not that it's visited much by rich connoisseurs, ho-ho.'

Q mumbles a diffident thanks. They continue chatting. About their year at the Schools together. Izzy as a part-time mature student. About Garth, a one-time business associate of the shambolic shopkeeper. And about the bald stripper, yet another acquaintance from Izzy's colourful past. A bell sounds. They return to the studio. Trundle along.
Side by side. Izzy towering over him.

Back.
In his galley.
At his oar.

The model, E.
The perceptor, Q.

Mass and tone.
Skin and bone. Chromatic flux.
Intraspace. Interspace. Metaspace.
Shapeshifting. Uncontrollably. Beyond logic.
Beyond the intervening photon field.
The brain, as neutron
poison.

How to reach and maintain critical mass.
How to trigger the exponential surge
to ontological meltdown,
when the best bubbles
are always blown.

Summon
the trenchers,

       the pile borers,
     the dragline excavators,

          paint, as live terrain,
          space, as creature,

          art, as war,
          life, as turmoil,
          the brush, as weapon.

The Difficult Cure.

The session
ends.

10.   **The Gallery**

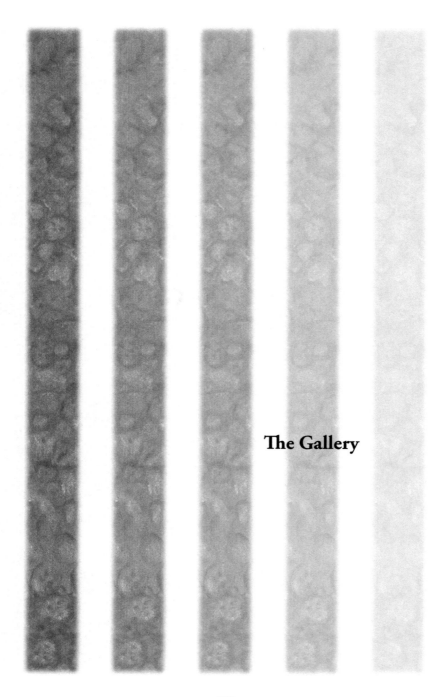

The Gallery

Diana.

Huntress ogre-belle.

Primed with zealotry and lye.

Jinxing ripples from the brook-flecked air.

Settles. Modulates. Moves in for the kill.

One breast bare. But more than bare.

Its pink-to-crimson bombazine has

gusted from her deathless flesh,

as burnt bark buckram from

a thunderbolted beech.

Actaeon.

Antlered ingénue.

Gash, and glyph, and metamorph.

Travestied and decked for death in fur and forest rot.

Pleads with all the leaf scrub, all the pipe-rust ivy.

For mediated caritas, the iron kiss of closure.

His hallowed hounds have impregnated

deep in him their chthonic canine law,

pressing pads and bloodied rags

into his disassembling core.

With the customary protocols of cleaning up and tidying away his painting clobber executed with robotic efficiency, the tyro has wolfed down his brie baguette, walked out of the Schools and hurried straight here.

He idolises Titian. Always has done. Ever since that afternoon when, as a dejected eleven-year-old, he first stumbled up the great stone steps of the National Gallery.

Seated before *The Death of Actaeon*.
Etching harsh, frightened lines into the face of his sketchbook.
Its mystery is endless, its intricately layered structure a miracle, its metaphysical narrative a stark invigorating adventure of which he never tires.

Ride.

Ride. Ride,

helmeted in hemlock, the climates of the sky.

Infiltrate the lit brindling of rough-roiled coppermelt.

Salute the hoary painter's buck-and-wing.

Observe the dread desuetudes of Fall

outgod the svelte velleities

of Spring.

'Hello, Q.

Hello…?

Q…?'

Dismounts.

Looks round.

There she is. Parked on the same broad bench as himself. With her back to him. Scrutinising *The Birth of the Milky Way*. The petroleum torrent of her hair is unmistakeable. Perversely in key with the overbearing sensuality of Tintoretto's melodrama. In need of a break from the hunter/huntress polemic, he shuffles around the bench to join the lowercase geometry of the witch's daughter.

'Hello Jaz. D'you like Tintoretto?'

'Not particularly,' she replies, snatching his sketchbook to glance at his drawing and returning it almost as quickly. 'I've just come from Poussin. *Landscape with a Snake.*'

'Love that picture. Is it part of your course?'

'No. I just like it. If that's alright with you.'

'Sorry. Didn't mean to patronise. But. You're...'

'So young? Oh well...'
Flashing him a dismissive scowl, she stands, picks her tiny rucksack up from the floor and marches off towards the old Trafalgar Square entrance.

Momentarily paralysed, he readjusts. Blunders after her. Marvelling as she thrusts her small body through the enormous glazed gallery doors. Past Piero, Botticelli, Mantegna, Giotto, the Lorenzetti Brothers. Down the carpeted stairs. Over the lobby floor mosaic and into the creaky revolving carousel of the main exit. On the balcony. Above the tourist-packed piazza. Catches up. Grabs her sleeve. 'Sorry.'

She pulls her arm free. Turns towards him. Covers her face with her half-pint hands, opening the fingers just enough for one dark eye to glisten through.

'You laughing at me?'

The hands drop from the face.
A rebellious smirk.

Adrift in the no-man's-land between annoyance and amusement, he directs a forensic look at the amber-hued features tilted so defiantly up at him. Heavy black eyebrows. Heavy-lidded, heavy-lashed eyes, with pupils black and intense as wet cherries. A small nose, somewhat off-kilter. A rangy mouth, supple and muscular, with the tiniest trace of a hare-lip. A shapely, decisive jaw.

Half and hour later they are strolling in St James Park. Beside the lake. Bidding *buonaserra* to the urban pigeons. Enjoying the long-shadowed company of ducks and crows, geese and sparrows, wing-clipped pelicans and self-maimed politicians. Talking about politics. Poetry. Music. Art. About Titian. Poussin. Delacroix. Cézanne. Bacon.

Agree and disagree. Mainly agree.

Laugh a little. Confess a little.

Unload a lot.

She is adopted. Her parents were killed when the Rolls driven by her drunk father crashed into a tree near Oxford. Six year-old Jasmine was in the back seat. Dragged from the wreck unconscious and in a coma for three weeks, she sustained brain injuries that even now cause her slight discomfort but which for several years after the accident led to wild and unpredictable rages. Her parents' house in North Oxford's academic ghetto was quickly sold off, and Belinda, her mother's sister and only surviving relative, became the sole beneficiary and the little girl's guardian.

Free from financial care, her aunt bought the cottage in the woods and gave up work as a contract nurse to devote herself to bringing up the fragile orphan. Partly for convenience and partly to blot out the memory of her alcoholic brother-in-law, she took the natural step of adopting her niece and changing the surname to her own. Q knew nothing of all this however, when at the age of fourteen he was told by local yobs that his father was shagging the notorious 'wood witch'.

He hung around the cottage for weeks after, spying on Belinda until finally he saw her kissing Garth in the porch. For a few days more he lurked, on-and-off, in the nearby bushes. Eventually he was spotted by Jasmine, who ran out of the cottage screaming at him to go away. He remembers striding towards her bellowing 'Your mother's a slut' over and over, again and again, before turning and rushing from the wood in bewilderment, undecided whether to tell his mother what the whole village already seemed to know.

On a bench.
By the lake.
In the park.

'How come the art connection?'

'My mother was a book illustrator and my culture-vulture father was always driving us up to London to see art shows. When he wasn't drunk, that is. We had loads of posh art books at home, which all came to Aunt Belinda after the accident. Mother liked to dump me in the Ashmolean while she went shopping in Cornmarket. I was only five but one of the attendants there would often talk to me about the pictures. That must be where I got up my love of Poussin. I still remember how fascinated I was by the Baby Moses painting, and that look, on the mother's face.'

'How extraordinary. At five I knew sod-all about art and cared even less, especially as my father only painted in his studio and never at home, which I couldn't understand and grew eventually to despise.'

A pair of geese waddle by.

'D'you know… there was a time when I thought you might be my half-sister? Because of that fling my dirtbag father had with your aunt. I was very angry. Should have done the maths of course, but…'

'I always wanted a brother. So perhaps I've got one now. Or not. No. Certainly not. I can't have a brother who sneers at Hockney. No way.'

'Well, I suppose the wheezy old bugger must be good at something besides smoking his filthy roll-ups – pulling the wool over the eyes of callow students perhaps?'

She punches him on the arm,
hissing with mock venom.

'So. Where in London will you be staying, little sister?'

'Less of the 'little', if you don't mind. Not too sure about the 'sister' either, come to that,' she laughs. 'In Highgate.

Off the Archway Road. I've my own decent-size room in a
basement flat, shared with two other girls. Both art students
as it happens. At the Slade.'

Mists and shadows
are usurping the park.

He wonders. About dinner.
With his new friend.
Decides against it.

'I must be off. You getting the Northern Line too?'

She nods.
They swap email addresses
and agree to meet up again soon.

Ambling out of the park.
Across Trafalgar Square.
Slowly. Still chatting.
Still laughing.

Up Charing Cross Road.
Into the station.

11.   Ecdysis

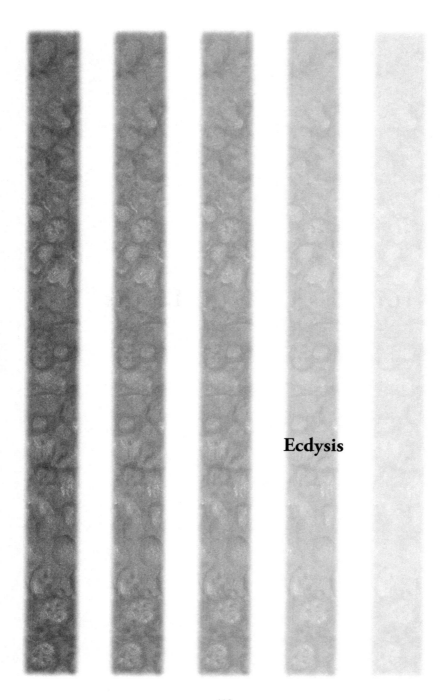

Ecdysis

Escalator.

Tufnell Park Station.

Onto the pavement. Stop.

Buy and stuff a kebabshop fishfingerburger

down his hungry gullet. Re-enter the station.

Board another train.

Back south.

To Soho.

Dom's Diner.

Eugène. Bestowing his default smile.

Q sits at the window, on the next barstool,

with coffee and a glass of water.

Drawing pen. Eraser.

Sketchpad.

Focus.

The no-entry sign, formerly an obliterated pest, becomes
pivotal. Its vertical ellipse hangs like an inked bass harmonic
over the lairy goose egg of the sex-shop window. He tinkers
with the four ovoids. Positioning. Re-positioning.

'Crap, I'm not here for this.'

Stow everything.

Pay the bill.

Skim across Old Compton Street.

Push open, once again, the mudbrown door.

Clamber, once again, up those glitzy fucking stairs.

She's still here.

Still in the spotlight. No-one else. No audience. No music. But fully clothed. In a black leather raincoat, belted and pocketed with the collar turned up, ready for the night. Counting out twenties into a diamanté purse. Snapping it shut. Dropping it into the Dior handbag at her feet, from which she retrieves, and then lowers onto her scalp, a bobbed auburn wig.

Adjusts it for symmetry.

'Can I help you?' she asks. Cool. Not unfriendly.

'Chlamydia, isn't it? Sorry to trouble you. My name's Williams. You may not remember but I rudely interrupted one of your performances here about six months ago. My sincere apologies for that. Izzy Higgs suggested I mention his name. He's a friend of mine. Says he knows you.'

'He knows me alright. And still owes me a tenner. The twerp with a trillion connections and sod-all common sense to monetise them. And Chloe's the name by the way. Another of his moronic jokes. So. How is the old bugger?

No. Don't answer that.'

The voice is deep, husky, without affectation. 'And of course I remember you. The Suicide Club finals.'

'Suicide Club…?'

'A peculiar bunch. Fifty contestants drawn from a pool of five hundred. Twelve finalists. Two winners. The first gets an executive-class return trip by private jet to Bangkok, six months' board and lodging in a five star hotel, plus a year's VIP subscription to the most luxurious and degenerate brothel in the whole of Thailand. The second gets all the right tools and instructions for a hassle-free legal euthanasia. My job is to shoot a paint pellet at whoever takes my fancy. Blue gets the brothel. Red gets the suicide. It's a knockout competition. From start to finish the whole palaver can take up to three hours. But it's only once a month. And money's money. Very lucrative it is too. Organised by the Garrick Club would you believe. And guess what…
There's a waiting list.'

'Bloody Hell…'

'Exactly. How can I help?'

He explains what brought him here in April. How the spooky figure from his father's stolen Bentley vanished. Somewhere. In this building. Offers her fifty quid.

'That's okay. I don't need it, and you're a friend of Izzy. But you missed the door I'm afraid. At the top of the stairs. The one before ours. No handles. No keyhole. Entry controlled by a state-of-the-art biometric security system. Eyeball recognition. It's the only way in to what I've heard is a vast network of soundproofed offices taking up most of the upstairs terracing on this side of Old Compton Street. Rough-looking suits come and go all the time on Tuesdays. But nothing much else. The landlord should be able to tell you a lot more. If you can persuade him. He's rich as Croesus. Works on reception in a crummy peepshow just round the corner in Frith Street. For one hour. First thing every other morning. He'll be there tomorrow. Some sort of convoluted double-bluff income tax dodge or so I gather. His name is Smythe. Deuteronomy Smythe. Looks like a hippy tramp. Long smelly hair. Long shaggy beard. Filthy old sandals. But don't be deceived. He owns half Soho.'

She stands.
Checks her reflection.

They leave,
together.

12.   Peepers

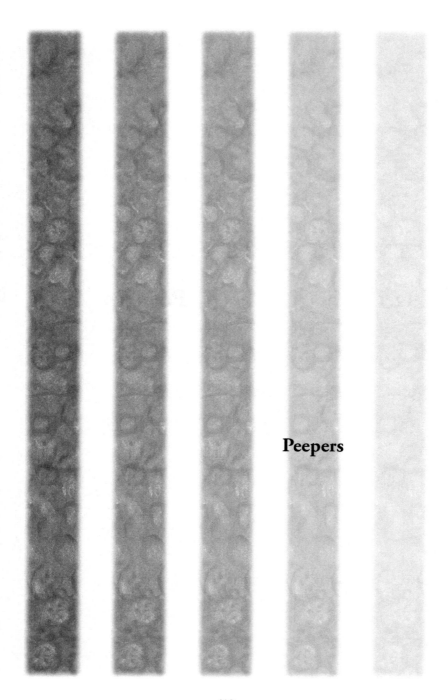

Peepers

Drizzle.

Frith Street.

Next morning.

Three differently bedraggled gents are inspecting the menus in the several and varied over-priced eating establishments dotted along the north end of the street. For the most part the fare as advertised is surely beyond their means.

The first of the aspirational hedonists to steal away from the dishes on offer is Genesis Crow, tall, overweight and anoraked. In his early twenties. Blonde and crew-cut all except for a single four-inch frond of luminous green dangling down over his left eye. Waddles across the street. Floats like a wayward zeppelin over the flashing neon-lit threshold of Peeping Tom's Tabernacle.

The worm-eaten threads of the second menuholic hang dejectedly from his body like seaweed from a derelict pier. Exodus Buñuel. The moist eighty-year-old eyeballs shuttle from side to side. Left right. Left right. Left right. Once his mind is made up, the elderly gent slinks rapidly across the glistening tarmac. Through the glistening doorway.

The third loiterer, Ludo Leviticus by moniker, is more at ease with himself, delighted to have engineered a compact half hour break into his busy middle management schedule. His eatery of choice adjoins the Tabernacle. After a discreet look round, he too vanishes. Imperceptibly.

In a blink. Like cheap stage magic.

Into the neon-edged portal.

In quick succession all three pass the reception desk, nodding to Deuteronomy Smythe, the frayed, extravagantly hirsute scarecrow on duty. None of them require any of the *Pound Coins Only* change on offer. Maintaining a wary distance from each other, they approach a narrow curving tunnel. Red ceiling. Red floor. Red walls. The tunnel's inner wall is punctuated every two metres by smutty, matt black firedoors.

Bulldozing through the first door,

Genesis Crow ducks his head. Slips inside. Rams home the bolt. Relieved to be blanketed at last in the warm squalor, he takes a little time to squint at some of the more legible flash-fiction scrawled on the walls. Fondling the crotch of his military camouflage chinos with one hand, with the other he drops five pound coins into a battered slot meter. Loosens his belt. Unzips his fly. The lid of his letterbox viewing window cantilevers up for the first ten minute session. The twitchy fingers of his dominant hand crawl sideways. Into his fly. Through the vent in his Y-fronts.

Around his semi-erect

member.

Wheezing audibly,

the antediluvian Buñuel heaves open the second door. Unfazed by his proximity to Crow, even pleased to have a younger version of himself to masturbate along with, he's looking forward to this, the only sensual extravagance and only significant human contact in his bleak and bootless life. His arthritic fingers fumble, missing the slot with his last pound coin. He sinks to his knees, gropes around on a floor still strewn with last night's wads of crumpled tissue. Finds his coin. Drops it in. Breathes an appreciative sigh as the letterbox lid creaks up. Yearning now for the desperately constrained eye-to-eye consolation that only this can provide, he lowers his head to the perspex window.

Confident and patient,

impeccable in his navy blue carcoat, Ludo Leviticus rocks on his feet. Waits till he hears the doors being closed on the first two customers. Exits the reception lobby. Glides gingerly through the tunnel, listening out for any sign of movement behind the doors. Eventually he reaches the last. It springs open to his touch. The stench is nauseating. Nonetheless he shuts and bolts the entrance to his chosen booth. Clears a tissue-free space on the floor with his shoe. Leans his leather briefcase against the partition. Extracts a pair of spectacles from his coat pocket and reads with considerable difficulty the instructions printed on the faded wall poster. Inserts his money. The flap cranks open.

A whore's boudoir.

Red satin. Black lace. Draped everywhere.

Purple candles flickering on every available surface.

Centre stage, a floor-to-ceiling dancing pole of glossy brass, uneasily close to the single bed, which is itself pillowless and mantled in crimson. The only picture is a long, gold-edged print of a saturnalian orgy. Fetishistic underwear is scattered around on the furry floor. Music begins. Low. Sinuous. Seismic. A curtain in the far corner jerks. Rhythmically. Almost, but not quite, in time to the music.

What comes crawling
through the satin curtain
are the unwashed naked feet
and the scrawny, grey-flannelled
back-end of Deuteronomy Smythe.

The recurrent jerkings, which might initially have been mistaken for a lascivious appetiser, have now grown crude and relentless. With each jerk the contour of the lugubrious receptionist displays a little more of itself through the thick curtain. Still more or less in time to the thumping music. And with each profound thump,
comes a short, sharp, but
increasingly emphatic
squeal.

Smythe is being kicked backwards, on all fours, by someone or something as yet undisclosed. Next comes the loosely cardiganned torso. Now the shoulders. Now the arms. Now the unshorn, blood-smudged head.

Still shuffling. In spurts.
To avoid the kicks.

The leprous body of William Blake's Nebuchadnezzar. Forcibly clothed and reincarnated. Into a rougher. Meaner. More terrified version of itself.

The heavy curtain is drawn aside to reveal the languorous shape of what appears to be a caped and masked simulacrum of the artist Eugène Delacroix. His black cape and mask are blazoned cryptically all over with miniature gold numbers. The dead painter's doppelganger kneels at the head of the grovelling victim. Asks a question.

The words of the question are lost
in the echoic rumble
of the music.

Smythe shakes his head. Shuts his eyes.
His interrogator grips an ear
in each hand.

Twists forward. Twists back.
Forward. And back. Many times.
Many times. In perfect synchrony
with the down-home rhythm
of the down-home blues.

Grubs
of bright crimson
peep out from the split hinges
of the Deuteronomy ear gristle.

He relents. Nods his head.
Speaks.

Time is up.
The scene freezes.
The music terminates.

The three flaps descend.
Slowly. In clamorous
uncoordinated
sequence.

13.   Beaches

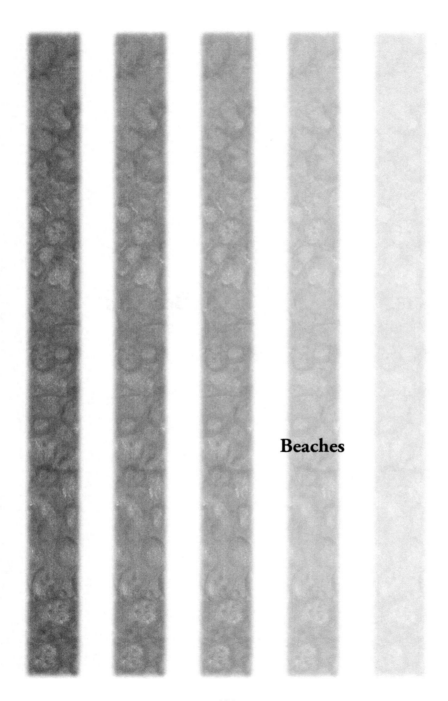

Beaches

The walk.
Down the hill,
from Brighton Station.

Convenience stores. Bureaux de change. Nondescript cafes.
Drab buses. Rapacious solicitors. Arrogantly artisan coffee
shops. All self-replicating on an endless loop.

The day is glum.
Mean. Unforgiving.
Which feels exactly right.

Thuggery.
Pure and simple.
Q recalls in disbelief the thud and scrape of boot on bone.
On the head. The face. On the brambly shoulders of the
unwashed, obdurately unaccommodating plutocrat.
Scrutinising his red-raw fist.
The fist, which floored.
Felt good, at the time.
Too good.

The palisades of grandiose hotels, grim offices and uppity
casinos have replaced the default dinge around the station.
Their extent and their height, as oppressive
as his shame and self-disgust.

And all this while.
Screened. In his skull.
Deuteronomy Smythe.
Squinting up, at him,
from the blooded rug.

Impenetrable.
Inviolate.

Did he really do all that?
Why couldn't he stop?
Where was Eugène?

Enough. Reboot. Forget.

Over the seafront road.
Down the concrete ramp.
Onto the beach.

He totters
in a half-dead trance
through the accusing stones
toward the beckoning swell.

Closer. Closer.
Closer.

A drugged
psychotic sky.
The sun and moon
look down, in their chains,
at crashing snowy waterfalls
of parasuicides and sea angels,
at punchdrunk, brainless rocks,
at putrid fish and zombie mermen.

Back. Back.
Scramble back.
Up the shelving shore.

Away from the inveterate
codependency of the exhausted gravel.
Away from the swirling multi-mirrored mist,
from the knuckledusting surf.

Up the ramp.
Over the pavement.
Through the iron gate.
Onto the wooden pier. Hot dogs.
Hamburgers. Doughnuts. Candyfloss.
Slats of doddery spruce.
Spray in his face.
A bench.

Beyond the Palace of Fun,
Mimi's bar, the Dome -
a smudge of seagulls.

Tiny red spider,
stroll across this
good hard pebble.

Sea, sea, finflap edge
of the world's flounder,

accept this poke of bones
into your cold, grey,

                          gut.

A whisper…

'Sorry I'm late.'

Q doesn't move.
His head is still drowning.
Still adrift in the churning dirt.

Down there.
Through the slats.
Under the pier.

'You okay?'

'Sorry Jaz.
Been a weird week.'

'Don't worry, I've been there myself. Quite a few times to be honest. Tell me.'

Little by little
she draws it out of him.
Soho. The Bentley. The Suicide Club. Izzy Higgs. Chloe the Stripper. The alienating trauma of his premeditated controlled violence on Deuteronomy Smythe.

'Don't lose any sleep over Smythe. I heard Garth discussing him once. On the phone. Nothing nice I can assure you. Odd you should know Izzy though.'

'You know him…?'

'One of my flatmates met him at a college exhibition. She invited him back for tea, a few weeks ago. Seedy piece of work. He came onto me an hour after we met. What a joke. He needs to improve his personal hygiene before putting himself about and leering at people like that.'

'He can be a clot. A letch too. But he's not all bad. Must've been drunk. I rather like him actually. He's somewhat unreliable, but he does have something. And he knows everyone. Quite bizarre. Why am I drawn to such flaky charmers? And vice versa, I have to confess.'

'So that's why you invited me here,' she laughs, punching his arm. Buys him candyfloss. Insists he eat it.
They fall into giggles. He feels better.
She asks what he learned.

'Quite a lot, in the end. The Old Compton northside terracing, over the shops, is filled with computers and used as a worldwide hacking and money-laundering hub for whichever criminal scumbags need the service. But more interestingly, the Eroticorium cellar contains the entrance to a secret underground passage which leads all the way to Burlington House in Piccadilly. The Royal Academy. My Alma Mater no less. Probably served as a fat-cat priest hole during the Civil War. The Academy end has been bricked up for centuries, but there's another way in. Some kind of service lift or dumbwaiter in the wine store of an up-market cocktail bar and restaurant in Air Street. *La Paloma*. That's where the new tunnel ends and the older bit to Soho starts. Apparently it's used to deliver considerable quantities of foodstuff and provisions, as well as the occasional crate of extremely bulky equipment.'

'Where to…?'

'Good question. He said he didn't know and I'm sure he told me all he could in the end. Poor sod. Can't believe I did all that. It was like someone else, not me. That's what I keep telling myself. Hope the disguise worked.'

The wind drops.
The waves have calmed.

The sun is setting
in a tamped down
tangerine sky.

They walk slowly
in a weird, bumpy kind of dance.
A serendipitously mis-matched pair.
Even for Brighton.

Q in blue.
Steady. Careful.
In a straight line.

Jaz in gold and black.
Bouncing around, like
a bee on uppers.

Over

the road.

Into Kemptown.

She knows the area well.

They enjoy a ditzy hotchpotch Belgian-style meal in the cellar
of a tiny music cafe run by a welcoming friend of hers.

A chilly walk

up to the station,

catching the train to Victoria.

And then the Northern Line tube,

taking leave of her on the Archway platform.

A hug.

A kiss on the cheek.

A good day. After all.

He hops on the train.

Southbound. Just one stop.

Back to Tufnell Park.

One hour later.

Midnight.

In his flat.

Drawing.

With pens. Inks.

Quarto sketchbook.

Mementoes of the day.

Above the pier, trick cacophonies of starlings converging, twisting in conveyor-belt ribbons across the darkening sky. Careening in pixelated arrows. Black crows quarrelling on the beach. Children playing in the waves, paddling in the foam at the sea's edge. The skeletal ghost of the burnt-out pier's heroic last stand, surrounded by the absurd piffle of five, or was it six, fluorescent windsurfers.

His phone rings.

Jaz. On video call.

In a street somewhere.

'Where are you?'

'At your front door. Waiting to be let in. With my overnight bag. Come on please, it's bloody cold out here.'

'Crikey. How d'you know I'd still be up?'

'You gonna let me in?'

'Just coming.'

He combs his hair in panic.

Finds his keys. Unlocks the door to his flat. Switches on the landing light. Descends the stairs two or three at a time. Unbolts the front door.

And there she is. On the pavement.

Small. Insignificant. In a pool of lamplight.

With her phone in one hand and a black holdall in the other.

And a strange expression on her face.

'What on earth you doing here?'

'I'll go if I'm not welcome.'

'Sorry, sorry. Do come in.'

She climbs the steps. Pushes past. He bolts the door behind her. In his flat, she drops the holdall on his table, takes off her duffel coat and throws it over the bag. Turns towards him. Thinks better of it. Sits on the double bed with her face in her hands. The stubborn sheen of her hair is the only message she is giving out.

'I'll leave if you want me to. I just thought that… after such a nice day… we should round it off with a nice fuck.'

She grins up at him.

'I'm serious.'

'Bloody hell. Can I get you a drink?'

'Just tapwater.'

He walks over to the sink. Turns on the tap. Fills a glass. Hands it to her. Fills the electric kettle. Switches it on. 'I'm making coffee. D'you want some?' She nods. He fumbles open a packet of chocolate biscuits. She takes one. Then another. Nervous, he busies himself with the elaborate coffee-making process. Grind the beans. Drop a filter in the ceramic cone. Empty the grounds into the filter. Place cone on mug. Pour on the boiled water. Wait.

When he turns round she is already in bed.
He takes the mugs to his bedside table.
Sits on the bed.

One minute, one biscuit,
and a mouthful of hot coffee later,
finds him under the duvet.

Beside her.

Both naked.

Their fingers lock.

'D'you do this often?'

'Only with you,' she smiles.

*   *   *

In a
dark alcove,
Eugène stands up.

Caresses his trim goatee.

Vacates the room.

Chuntering.

14.   *La Paloma*

La Paloma

Two days later.

5.30am. Pin Place.

A narrow cul-de-sac.

Off Air Street. Near Piccadilly.

Cold. Dark. Damp.

LA PALOMA : Staff Entrance.

Casual Kitchen Staff often required.

Assemble here at 6.00am – Tuesdays only.

Permanent positions for suitable candidates.

He saw the notice last night

on his way back from the Schools.

Twenty or so hopefuls have shown up to form a disorderly queue behind him. All men. At least half are winos. Most of the others are either too scruffy or too long in the tooth. Only one seems about his own age, whether student or drifter is hard to say, especially in this light and with everyone wrapped up against the weather. But he looks friendly and is next in the queue. 'What's the job?' Q asks. The job is part-time. Three days a week. Huddled together in the drizzling murk, they start chatting.

He's Hugo. A thirty-year-old writer from York.

Pale, long-haired and lean, he earns his crust as a part-time teacher and occasional dishwasher. After bumbling his way through the schools and kitchens of the Midlands and the Home Counties, he's ended up in Camden. He adores Whitman, is widely read in the western poetry canon, including all of the Divine Comedy, most of Milton and much of Blake, can happily recite long chunks of Shakespeare by heart, and loves the prose of Dickens. And Joyce. And Borges. The young artist can't believe his luck.

After an hour's standing and talking and growing colder by the minute they smile with relief as the double doors open. A grey-suited, grey-skulled, grey-weskited skeleton looms above them. In the doorway. The likeliest looking five, including Q and his new companion, are chosen and ushered into the panelled lobby. All five are lined up against the wall and told the restaurant requires just two casuals this week. Once the skeletal apparatchik has spoken to everyone and checked their IDs, Hugo and Q are hired as kitchen porters. He escorts the failed applicants outside, introduces himself as Nathaniel Tebbit the Duty Manager, and gives the winning pair a brief tour of their workplace. From the dim lobby they're led along a bright, many-doored cream corridor, and thence into the three main Dining Rooms and the enormous Kitchen.

Food is stored in the basement and delivered there by means of a large dumbwaiter near the entrance. It's large, Q is thinking, but nowhere near big enough to carry the elephantine crates of provisions and heavy equipment down to the Burlington Tunnel as so painfully described by Deuteronomy Smythe.

Leading them down to the storage areas, Tebbit explains that until the regular staff arrive their job will be stacking the new deliveries. The nexus of lower storage spaces is known as the Larder, consisting of four Storage Rooms, the Wine and Cask Cellars, and the Refrigeration Pods. He supplies them with a broom each. Then it's back up to the lobby with orders to sweep the black and white tiles of what appears to be a perfectly clean floor. He leaves them to cope alone. A brewery van arrives. Casks and kegs are dealt with by the draymen. Bottles and cans are loaded into the dumbwaiter and sent below to be sorted and stacked later.

For the first hour they are by themselves. But no more deliveries. Q seizes his chance and examines every niche, nook and cranny of the Cellars but finds no sign of any lift, secret or otherwise.

They talk non-stop, Hugo telling his tale in bits and scraps. A dropout from sixth form, he went to work with a builder friend for three days a week with the intention of writing and educating himself away from the academic drool of his teachers. It didn't quite work out like that, but it did give him plenty of time to study and do his own writing. Then, after just one year, he saw his friend plummet from a barn roof in the Yorkshire Dales miles from anywhere, and had to wait as the poor guy died in agony from internal bleeding before the ambulance showed up. Following that, Hugo's life went awol for a time, but eventually he pulled himself together, decided to finish his A levels at night school, and slogged away for a couple more years at his teaching degree. He now does his own writing and keeps the financial hyena from the door with temporary teaching work plus low-paid menial jobs like this one.

'Took a while to sort myself out. But here I am. In London. On my third novel. None of them published. Some interest in the first. Didn't bother with the second. Won't bother with the third either.'

'Don't understand. Why do it, Hugo? It's a lot of work.'

'Doesn't make sense does it. But I'm creating a world. Where anything can happen.' He grins. 'It's the adrenaline, I guess. What I live and breathe for.'

At 11.30 they are joined by the regular porters and sent to the Kitchen, where they toil as skivvies, cleaning up after the chefs, hacking off cauterised gunk from the steel frying pans ready for the heavy-duty dishwasher, loading and unloading both machines, handwashing any items too hefty or fragile for the dishwashers, and lugging out heavy bags of rubbish to the dumpster.

At 2.30 they are paid off in cash by Tebbit and instructed to return at the same time tomorrow. 'Does this mean we've permanent jobs? Or is it just his way of keeping us guessing?' muses Hugo, as they drop down the steps
into Piccadilly Station.

Q says nothing.
His head is filling up with Jaz.
And wondering...

Elizabeth Street.

Up the steps.
Unlock the door.
Mrs Schrödinger. In the hall.
Dusting. Two black kittens playing around her feet.
As soon as he's shut the front door, she slips the duster into her apron pocket and picks up the kittens, clasping them to her matriarchal bosoms. 'Would you like to stroke them?' she enquires with a repugnant leer.
He scratches both kittens,
briefly, on the head.
Retreats upstairs.

At least she didn't see Jaz leave yesterday morning.

But why should that be a problem?

Locks his door.

Starts to phone Jaz.

Remembers she has lectures.

Decides to work on his painting.

Sets up.

The canvas.

Tall and narrow.

A view of the sex shop facing Dom's Diner.

A dark night. A car. Parked before the oval windows.

In the back seat, a silhouette of uncertain size or gender.

The top half isn't right.

He works on it for an hour.

Observed,

      from a corner,

           by Eugène.

He phones Jaz.

Describes his not entirely fruitless day in *La Paloma*.

Asks about her own day. Two classes. The first, in the morning, on Egyptian architecture, its origins and demise. The second, on Palladio. In Venice. All good.

They agree to meet up soon. She invites him for dinner at her place in Highgate on Thursday. He accepts and says a cheerful goodnight. Pours himself a brandy. Reads twelve wild and worrying pages from *The Aleph,* by Borges.
Cleans his teeth. Sets his alarm.
Climbs into bed.
Falls asleep.

5.15.
The alarm.

Crawl out of bed.
Take an extended pee.
Breakfast. Tea. Toast.
And into the shower.
Clean underwear.
Shave.

Hit the street.
More light rain.

On the grass verge
a club-clawed pigeon dunks grizzled nuggets of stale cake and fresh bread into a kerbside rill, as the filthed, beaten jowls of a white builder's van
hunker by.

A worried mother, with a buggy in tow. Staring out over the railings. Waiting for the lights to change. And then. Not moving. When they do.

Into the station. Catch the tube
to Leicester Square.

La Paloma.
Hugo. Here already. Rings the bell.
The door is opened by Tebbit, who gives them a mop and broom each with orders to clean the floor after last night. 'What happened last night?' whispers Hugo. The tiles of the chessboard floor are smeared with dirt and strewn with pellets of brown cardboard. The cadaverous Duty Manager deposits a large pail of hot soapy water at their feet.
And walks off.

The lobby is high and spacious, panelled floor-to-frieze in varnished oak. Above the dado, in each square panel hangs a massive oil painting. Six pastiches of done-to-death biscuit-tin lollipops by John Constable. Facing them is a version of Tate Britain's *Hadleigh Castle*. Q is studying it with a mixture of admiration and ennui when he notices what looks like a dog's-head-shaped button. Bottom left. Where the actual dog's head should be.
He touches it.

The whole panel, from floor to picture rail, clicks and jerks out. Just a fraction. He prods the carved and gilded frame. It clicks back. Looks for a button on the opposite side. Sure enough, there it is. Shaped to resemble a clod of earth. Invisible. Unless you're looking for it.

Hugo is sweeping the floor nearby.

In his own world.

'I'm off to explore. Is that okay? Won't be long.'

Hugo agrees, with diffidence, to cover for him.

Q presses both buttons.

The panel springs out a full inch.

Hooks his fingers under the frame. Pulls.

The panel hoicks towards him on its vertical hinge to reveal another room. A smaller, dingier version of the entrance lobby. Doorless. Windowless. With different copies of the same six paintings on the walls. The panel he's just come through is blank on this side. Closing it behind him, he notes that the buttons are precisely where they should be. But clear and undisguised. The fakes in this chamber are, without exception, poor in quality.

On the opposite wall, an inept copy of the Royal Academy's *Leaping Horse* is of particular interest. He searches for and discovers two more buttons of similar size. And position. And invisibility. Presses them. The panel clicks open to disclose yet another clandestine room. Even smaller. And the walls are empty. No pictures. Facing him is a pair of heavy mahogany doors. But locked.

Five minutes later he has returned through the secret rooms and re-entered the main lobby. Hugo is still there. Mopping the floor. 'Any deliveries?' asks Q.

'No. What did you find?'

He describes in copious detail the secret chambers and the locked doors. Hugo is intrigued. Stops mopping. Suggests he might be able to help with the doors. It so happens that only last week he was given a bunch of lockpicks by his twin sister, just engaged to a reformed and newly Christianised thief and housebreaker.

Deciding to trust his fledgling pal, Q divulges everything he's learned about the legend of the Burlington Tunnel and the supposed lift down to it.

Hugo searches his bag. Does he have the picks with him? He does. The pair skivvy away until lunchtime, are paid off in cash by Tebbit, instructed to return at the same time tomorrow and left to make their own way out.

Loitering in the lobby,

pretending to be busy on their phones, they are in fact ensuring that no-one's around. So they can slip, unseen. Into...

Now...

Easing open the panel, they make anxious progress through the three dud chambers to the locked doors. Hugo tries his picks. The last one works.

Through the doors and into a narrow ante-room. Before them is an enormous lift with a brass-handled gate left invitingly open. Its walls are lined with scuffed and dented stainless steel, its dimensions are those of a small shipping container. Q is pleased, but postpones further exploration.

Re-locking the doors, making their way back to the entrance lobby, they arrive at the last panel. Hugo looks up. Points to a long monitor installed above the picture rail.

The screen is split into three.

A view of the entrance lobby.

A view of the cream corridor.

A view of the street outside.

In the lobby, they spot Tebbit,

hanging around, yawning.

Checks the time
on a gold stopwatch,
nods to himself and
strides in haste across
the chessboard floor.

Out.

Nervous,
the intruders
release the panel.

Close it carefully.
Glide over the tiles.
Open the main door.

Scuttle into the street.

Lock the
lock.

15. The Mews

The Mews

Home.

In his flat.

On his phone. 'Hello, Jaz.'

'Hello, mister. How was your day?'

'Complicated. I'm really sorry, but is there any chance of me coming round for dinner this evening, instead of tomorrow? I need to talk.'

'Okay. My flatmates are out tonight, so that should be fine. Yes of course. Any time after seven.'

'Thanks. Appreciate it. Soon after seven.'

'See you.'

Clean shirt.

Spruce up a bit.

Down the stairs.

Out the front door.

Tube.

To Archway.

Up the escalator.

Out the ticket hall.

Wait at the windy bus stop.
Or walk. Plenty of time.
Walk.

Across the pedestrianised road. On past the ghost of what he remembers as the windiest bus stop in North London. Into the Archway Road. Past the Whittington Nurses' Barracks. Past another windy bus stop. Ahead lours the infamous but handsomely wrought Archway Bridge, which takes the Hornsey Lane traffic high over the Archway Road and then across to Waterlow Park and Highgate Village.

A lorry thunders past.
A sparrow drops out of the sky.
At his feet. Mangled conker head.
Half-blown-away by a shotgun pellet.

A shadow. He looks up. Before him stand a matching pair of skittle-like emo girls – clad in ash – hair combusted to obsidian spikes – they ask their question – then go.

Steps around the dead sparrow.
Up the hill. Leaden cliffs. Both sides.
Under the suicides' favourite bridge. Dodges the phantom fallers. Hurries on past the manicured Church of Saint Barnabas of Highgate and Paddington. Over the busy highway. Past Tyrion's Bolt Hole and Hodor's Kitchen.

Calls in the shabby off-license to buy a mid-range bottle of Tempranillo. On past the Boogaloo Pub with its boogaloo music, its boogaloo décor and its boogaloo staff. Pauses at the Murakan Hindu Temple to take in the sparkly new statues of Shiva and Ganesh.

Here.
Here it is.
Below the Archway Road.
Lembury Mews. A secluded, tree-lined sanctuary.
Down a bank of steps. Into the avenue of Victorian terraces. Their deep basements make the houses look taller than they appear from the main road. And then he finds it.
32a. A basement flat. Down more steps.
To his right, a steep, cosseted rosebed.
Facing him, a purple door.
No knocker.
No bell.

The door opens.
And there she stands.
In a black and gold dress and long shiny earrings. Looking up at him, her face one big smile. 'Saw you on the steps,' she says. They kiss. Embrace. She feels warm and homely. 'I hope you don't mind but it's just a ready meal.'

'Of course not. Apologies for the short notice but I need to talk face-to-face. I might have blundered. Trusting someone I've only just met. And don't worry about the ready meal. It'll go with the plonk I've brought.'

Hands her the bottle.

She leads him through the silky aubergine hallway into a tousled, ultra-bohemian sitting room with a low round coffee table mantled by a richly woven, Mayan-style shawl. On the hennaed walls are the usual mix of exhibition posters, from Klimt to Klee to Kandinsky. Plus a few classic film images, *Metropolis*, *Amélie*, *The Third Man*, etc.

He sits down on an over-cushioned Egyptian sofa while she sees to the food. Tells her about Hugo. The secret rooms. The giant lift. The 'coincidence' of the bunch of lockpicks. 'What are the chances?'

'Coincidences do happen. But yes, I agree. Unlikely. What do you know about him?'

'Not a lot. We talked about poetry and writing. And generally agreed. But I know almost nothing about his background, other than he's from up north, and a part-time teacher and jobbing labourer. Mind you, he is well read and appreciates loads of fine writing, which I'd normally take as a pretty good indicator of personal integrity. Also he has excellent taste in modern art and an eclectic love of all kinds of music. A bit like me in fact.'

'Have you read any of his fiction? Poetry can mean many things to many people, but with fiction it's harder to hide. He's on his third novel you say?'

'Absolutely no idea what it's about. Nor what style it's in. Nor where it's coming from. Said his first was partly autobiographical.'

'That doesn't tell us anything. Seems to me you have to go for it. No real choice. I'll come along with you if you like.' She hands him the bottle of wine. 'Can you open this while I lay the table for what I can't guarantee will be one of the most exciting meals of your not-very-long but moderately productive life?'

Crossing to the worktop, he unscrews the bottle and pours two large glasses. She lays out china ramekins filled with sweet chilli hummus and home-made guacamole. Opens a box of seeded beetrooty breadsticks. Drops a handful into a black vase on the Mayan coffee table.

She raises her glass.
He raises his.

They play games
with the fancy starter.

She walks over to the fridge.
Takes out the chilled dinners.

The penne chicken arrabiata portions
are microwaved. And then decanted,
along with a modest avocado salad,
onto stoneware dinner plates.

They sit at the hippy table.
Drink the hippy wine.
Eat the hippy food.
Converse a little.
Laugh a lot.

And then he leaves.
Busy day ahead.
After all.

16.   Prelude

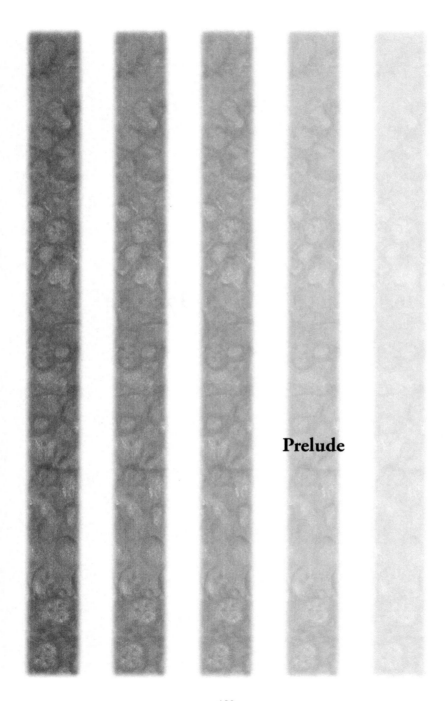

Prelude

Lunchtime.

Caffè Nero, Piccadilly.

A cavernous low-ceiling basement.

Two. In a corner. Hidden by a square pillar hung all over with brags and imprecations. *Best espresso this side of Milan. All coffee freshly ground minutes before serving.*

A tall, black-haired and balding barista is clearing up cups and mugs and plates and cutlery into a plastic washing-up bowl. Wiping the tables with his hairy-backed hands. 'Hello, young Q,' he chirrups, spotting one of his regulars sequestered in a huddle with a man he can't see.

'Hi Jonathan,' comes back the mumbled reply. Jonathan takes the hint. Moves away to deal with abandoned crockery and metalwork in the far corner, under a massive printed blow-up of a card game being played by a quartet of hugely wise and wizened Italianate faces, each mired deep in its own brown and philosophising study.

On the opposite wall. Another print of similar size but even greater enlargement of a gigantic newly drained espresso cup, with a brace of two-metre-long, elegantly fingered and opulently jewelled female hands, hovering above,
in alert proximity.

Below the giant cup.

Hugo. In conversation with his new workmate.

'The early hours are our best bet. It'll be risky but once inside the secret chambers we'll be as free from disruption as we're ever likely to be. And yes, of course Jaz can come. Be an excuse if we're caught. Studenty pranks.

Magistrates love them.'

The long fingers are pointing down. A raucous mob of sapphire and ruby rings are crammed together on the inner digits of both hands. Chanting. Denouncing. The empty cup would comfortably hold three human heads. With plenty of room for an equal amount of extremely hot coffee.

But Q is looking elsewhere, beyond Hugo.

A pair of crimson suede boots has appeared at the top of the stairs. They start walking down. Black tights. Red jacket. Black and gold dress. Red necklace. A turbulent cascade of glossy black hair. She trots over. Kisses Q. After a brief introduction and exchange of greetings with Hugo, Jaz sits down to discuss arrangements for the coming night.

The balding barista has vanished upstairs
with his bowl of dirty dishes.
They are alone.

17. The Tunnel

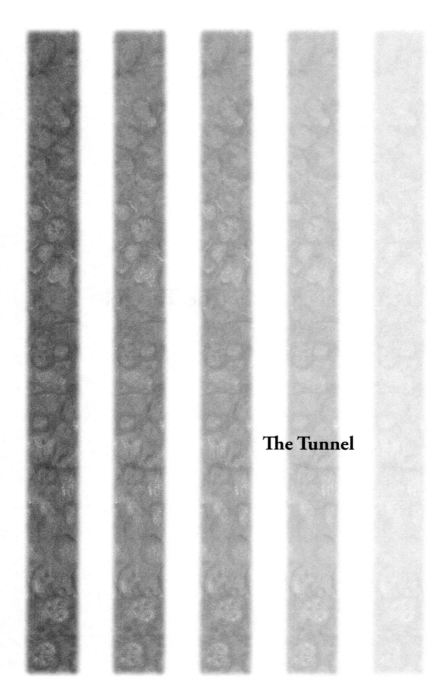

The Tunnel

Night.

The smallest hour.

Four silhouettes.

Converging on Seven Dials.

Convening in the Soho Arts Club doorway.

Street sleepers all around. 'Where are they from,' rasps Jaz, 'and where do they go?' Q and Hugo shrug their shoulders. The fourth shape, Eugène, hangs back from the others, murmuring something inaudible

to everyone but himself.

Hugo looks round.

Sees nothing.

The group weaves its way through the mass of frayed bodies. None of them objects, despite being intermittently stumbled over by three of the four. They are evidently used to it. Eugène, at the rear, floats over everything.

Through

the labyrinth

of living corpses.

And into Pin Place.

No rough sleepers here.

La Paloma. A bright light
floods the tradesman's entrance.

They cluster round.
Hugo tries his picks on the great door.
No problem. Not even an alarm.
Into the lobby.
Unseen.

Jaz watches
as Q nudges the buttons
on *The Hay Wain*, pulling
and teasing open the panel.

Through the dull
fake-filled chambers
steal the four intruders.

Into the industrial lift.
Closing the doors behind them.
Drawing together the brass gates.

High above their heads
a twelve-bulb spotlight-bar
spans the length of the ceiling.
The bulbs start to flicker.
Q frowns.

Jaz pushes a button.
Eugène nods his approval,
unseen by all
except Q.

The gate clatters shut.
The lift descends.
Without noise.

After what seems like several minutes
but is in reality less than one
they touch the bottom.

The gate clatters open.
The double doors facing them are panelled like those above
but coated in wrinkled bituminous varnish. They ease them.
Gently. Wide open. And walk out. Into fug.
A sweet viscoid mephitis. Fresh soot.
Old burning.

The light is feeble.
Feebler than in the lift and the chambers above.
A ten-metre-wide rotunda. With blackened walls and an ash-
caked ceiling. From which hangs a barely legible notice:

Piccadilly Loading Terminus

Confronting them and hogging most of the space stands an iron-wheeled box-barrow made of rough beechwood. Shoulder-high and half the length of a railway carriage, on narrow gauge steel tracks. The walls of the vehicle are badly charred. A new plywood floor has been laid, but only a stopgap trellis-type framework of struts and battens is in place to protect fresh cargo from the cauterized walls. The driving seat bolted to the front also looks new, along with its associated control panel and LED screen, alive and flashing and ready to go.

The paltry illumination dribbles from hyphenate threads of tubed neon attached to the roof. An up-to-date sprinkler system has been installed. The only exit is through a burnt square-beam portico. They follow the track through the portico as it curves down the shallow gradient before emerging into what must surely be the Burlington Tunnel. Free at last from the overpowering stench of incinerated timber, they look around in awe.

To their left stretches the Tunnel.
With its lofty slate-lined walls, vaulted ecclesiastical ceiling and dust-thick Yorkstone floor, the architecture has an empty, echoing uniformity. Monotonous, to the point of intimidation. Third Reichian.
Brutalist.

The silver rails continue for a long mile through the gloom. Far away in the distance shimmers a nebulous green glow. Which makes no sense at all.

To her right Jaz spots a tiled and cobbled miniature cave, little more than a burrow, which presumably leads to Soho and must be all that remains of the original seventeenth century priest-hole. She peels off, for a closer look. On entering even she has to bend her head to avoid the jagged granite of the ceiling. The blue and ivory tiles are in excellent condition. Primitive Dutch Delft, she guesses. Of superb craftsmanship considering the volatility of the political climate when the tunnel was constructed. She wants to explore more deeply. But.
'Focus,' breathes Q.

The rails run along the far side of the mall, leaving a spacious boulevard for pedestrians. The group moves on.
In silence. To the green glow.

After a few minutes the compacted geology of the ground above begins to stir, to groan, to grumble. A tube train. The grumble swells to a roar and finally becomes so loud that it seems the train itself must be in the tunnel heading straight for them. They look round.
Nothing.

The racket subsides.
Is replaced by a murmur of voices,
the sounds of shuffling, of walking.

Out of the Soho priest-hole, in a meandering file of twos and threes, an army of negro miners comes trundling towards them. Dressed in cream boiler suits, red wellingtons and yellow helmets. Shouldering worn pick-axes and battered sledge hammers. Their boots and boiler suits are smeared all over with scumbled patchworks of grey-brown mud. Their black faces are rilled with sweat and white dust.
Their eyes are tired, hurt and angry.

A squad of hardnose caucasian guards, armed with wooden cudgels and uniformed in royal blue, have been posted at regular intervals to keep the column moving.

'Hell,' snarls Q as he drags Jaz and Hugo out of the way, their backs pressed against the wall to allow the procession sufficient leeway. Eugène floats to the other side.

The miners draw level.

And stream past.
Jostling one another for no obvious reason. They are made up of all ages, mostly rough-looking men, with a few adolescent boys, a few dotards and a sprinkling of hefty women. One

of the older men, with thin grey hair and a straggly beard, stumbles and trips. He falls cursing to the ground and causes a local commotion. This is soon resolved when he is set upon and bludgeoned to death by two of the guards. The assailants drag the corpse to one side. The march past continues uninterrupted.

Despite the constant murmur of voices, no-one can be seen actually talking. All are locked in their own private spaces. And no smell. No footprints in the dust.

The cortege is endless.
Its leaders are now a hundred metres ahead, while at the rear the file is still pouring out of the small tunnel. None of the workers has acknowledged or even noticed the four white interlopers, who continue their journey in single file, keeping a comfortable gap between themselves and the disgruntled procession.

Another train rumbles through the ground above them. Quiet. Then loud. Then very loud. Then quiet again. Then nothing.

Suddenly.
An ear-splitting crackle.
The queue of miners vanishes.

And reappears.

Little more than a blink.

And seconds later. Another loud crackle.

The blink reoccurs, followed by a staccato of identical crackles during which the whole company of at least five hundred workers vanishes completely. Without trace.

'Was that a hologram?' croaks Jaz.

At this point they are fifty metres from the green haze, which is now even more intense, but still has no obvious explanation.

The tyro is thinking, speculating.

The electromagnetic quanta which must in theory constitute the wall of shimmering light, appear to pour down from the tunnel roof in multi-hued stripes or ripples of a harsh, stabbing brilliance. When glimpsed on the outermost edge of the visual field however, the ripples deliquesce into a level plane, which gradually changes its chromatic structure.

But with no consistency.

From olive to jade from jade to emerald.

From emerald to sage. From sage to sea green.

From sea green to chartreuse. And so on.

It makes no sense.

He wonders if it might be some kind of optical conjuring trick similar to the holographic miners' procession. Maybe this is what the whole Burlington Tunnel thing is about and his father's connection to it immaterial or coincidental.

As they approach the glare it grows fiercer, impossible to look at for more than a glance. The steel rails disappear into it with no hint of their continuance beyond. They hesitate. Common sense tells them that the motorised wagon carrying provisions and materials must pass through the light without in any way damaging its cargo, be it animal, vegetable or mineral.
But.

A giant,
ecologically incongruous hornet
has been pestering Jaz for quite some time.
Buzzing around her head. Putting an end to her chat with Hugo. She bats it away. Towards the wall of light. To her surprise the hornet flies straight into the wall and vanishes. And then reappears out of it twenty seconds later. Unharmed. Not in the least aggrieved.

'Let's go through,' she proposes. 'The hornet survived, we're sure to be fine.' She enters.
Followed by the men

On opening their eyes,

they find themselves submerged in a warm lustre.

Beset by gently falling flakes of a golden translucent snow.

Squinting through the flakes,

they have passed into an immense circular antechamber. An unloading bay of fifty metres diameter with smooth pink walls broken only by two pairs of enormous panelled doors of unequal size and ten metres apart.

Beneath their feet

stretches a lawn of soft vivid green which at first appears synthetic but is in fact quite natural and dotted with clusters of wildflowers. Small patches of daisies and forget-me-not are interspersed with many plants unknown to any of them, even Jaz, who claims some expertise.

Flowering shrubs have been planted at modest distances from each other. Inordinately curious, she spots a diminutive blue beehive secreted behind two bushes of ornamental cherry, presumably home to the battalion of honey bees now busying themselves in the wildflowers around her feet.

She ambles over to investigate. Tries not to annoy the bees but disturbs instead a magnificent peacock butterfly, in addition to innumerable nervy grasshoppers.

The steel rails crawl out from under the green light barrier and continue through the grass onto a wedge-shaped flagstone patio in front of the doors. Over the smaller exit hangs a triangle of yellow plastic, engraved with the words:

SCIENCE
A.I. Research.
Advanced Kinetics.
Electro-Photo-Synthesis.
In-Depth Hyper-Holography.

And over the larger doors,
another yellow triangle,
engraved in rust.
One word:

ART

The air is fragrant.
Slightly damp. And the light diffuse. Not too bright.
Looking up, they can discern neither ceiling nor roof structure through the diaphanous glimmer.

A dragonfly lands
on Hugo's arm.
Flies off.

And still.

Still

the downpour from the ersatz sun.

Still

the gilded flakes of photon.

Still

falling.

Still
no sight,
still no sound,
of real, live, human beings.

Reasoning that beyond both sets of doors there is bound to
be some kind of human activity and that opening either will
result in blowing their cover once and for all,
they agree to stick together.

But which doors first?

Q suggests
the smaller set,
the doors marked:

18.   *Science*

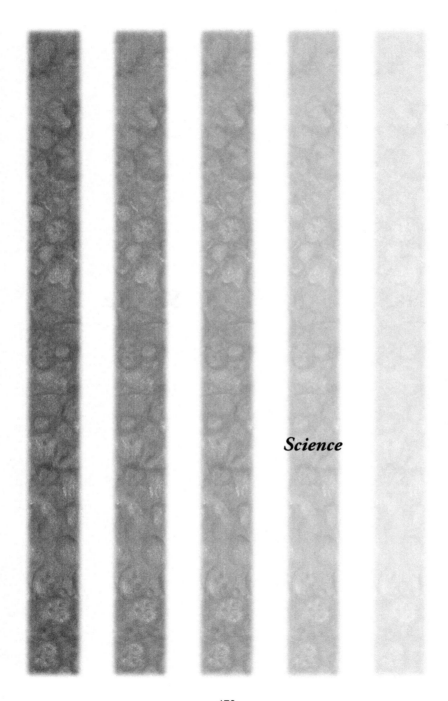

Science

178

press here   *press here*

Satin-silver.

Oblong buttons.

Either side of the frame.

The tyro

presses one.

The doors open.

Facing them

blocking the way

is a plate glass screen,

three metres square, dense,

milky-opaque, with black metal legs

and a thick black frame.

Etched onto the glass,

taking up 90% of the surface,

a schematic of square symbols,

particles of matter and energy,

mauve Quarks, green Leptons,

pink and yellow Bosons…

**THE STANDARD MODEL
OF ELEMENTARY PARTICLES**

Behind the glass.

Beyond the haze. A movement.

A pallid sphere, no bigger than a football.

Hovering. Drifting. Horizontally. To the right.

Traversing the screen. Through the Quarks...

the *down*, the *strange*, the *bottom*.

Leaving the chart altogether.

Across the milky border.

Up to the black metal.

Around the edge.

Floating in their general direction

with a nonchalant grin

on its gaunt

flushed

face,

comes

a detached

human head.

Stephen Hawking.

On a stiff white doyley.

'Good morning, mi amici,' announces the impudent monotone, idly sauntering through the elastic hoop of his lips. The timbre is that of a coldly mechanical voice generator, in no way mollified by its transatlantically extenuated vowels.

'Welcome to the Science Hub.

Level nine. The Eco-Processor.'

The head drops.

Without warning.

To Jaz's height.

Eye to eye.

Startled, she grabs the nearest arm. Hugo's. Befuddled by the accelerating weirdness, the writer panics. Frees his arm. Totters backwards. Into the double doors. Hands stretched behind him. His fingers scrabble at panels.

Find nothing. No escape.

The Hawking head smiles. 'Don't worry Hugo. You'll be out soon.' Still smiling, it beckons. With its eyes. Floats away from the screen. Out. Into the open.

They follow.

Onto a broad latticework shelf,

girdling the bowels of a vast octagonal Galleria.

The construction throughout is of ornately engineered stainless steel. The cloister-dome ceiling is adorned with filigreed pictograms of coloured crystal and hung with a kaleidoscope of Murano chandeliers. The inner edge of the shelf is secured by an Art Nouveau fence of chromium steel.

Jaz leans over the rail.
Looks down. Taking it all in.
A deep pit with cambered walls
ringed with lines of shelving
identical to their own.

She counts eight more levels.
Eight concentric octagons checkerboarded with screens and
control panels, all operated by diminutive robots of brightly
polished silver and varying heights. Headless. None taller
than a twelve-year-old adolescent.

The octagons diminish in diameter the lower she looks,
the lowest being no more than ten metres across, beneath
which lies a mosaic floor devised as a map of the northern
hemisphere, with an enormous jade egg
revolving, picaresquely,
at its centre.

'Come,' says the head as it glides over the platform. 'The name's
Stephen by the way. I'm your designated guide. You've just left
the Central Europe Eco-Shell, our Primary Unloading Bay,
one of six Shells on this level, each with its own micro-climate
and each customised to simulate a different region of Planet
Earth. The dashboards by the doors are all the same. Their
dials calibrate the seasonal changes in temperature, rainfall,

sunlight and humidity. With all calibrations pre-set, they don't require the attention of our robots, unless a particular experiment is in progress. There are none at present.'

They hurry past the doors labelled *North Africa, The Russian Steppes, The Arizona Desert.* Each time declining their guide's invitation to explore. Finally arriving at a vertical ladder. Bolted to the wall. Through square apertures cut into the latticework shelving, the ladder descends all the way down to the mosaic floor.
With so many levels,
Q is impatient.

He bids the head
a polite farewell.
Leads the group
down the ladder.

They are received,
to their consternation,
by another hovering headpiece
of the quirkily genial cosmologist.

'Hello again. Welcome to level eight. This level and those below it are the digital building blocks of the Particle Physics Centre. Each matrix of screens and panels is connected to the Primary Detector of one of the six most powerful Particle

Accelerators in existence, from the SuperKEKB in Japan to CERN's Haldron Collider on the Swiss border. The proton collisions in the accelerators are replicated here, and the resultant data collated and stored. Any questions?'

'Yes,' says Q. 'Do you or any of your other heads know of a man called Garth Williams? He's an artist. And lecturer. Looks like me. But shorter. With bigger hair.'

'Sorry, I'm afraid not. Unless he's disguised as a robot. Which would be extraordinarily problematic.'

They look round, studying in turn each of the dozen shiny robots on this level, all focussed on their screens, on their control panels. Different heights but the same design. Two short legs. Squat torso. Four long arms, one pair connected to each shoulder. Eight attenuated fingers per hand. A single electronic eye, glinting from the centre of every oversize palm.

Eugène is bored.
Leans over the fence.
Gazes at the levels below.

Hugo meanwhile has wandered further along the platform and is peering over the shoulder of one of the robots as it makes adjustments to a rack of monitors. He gulps as the images come into focus. On every screen. In explicit, high definition close-up. Pyrotechnic orgies of flesh and fur and genitalia. Culminating in simultaneous volleys of viscid ejaculations. Multiple cameras. Varying viewpoints. Dumbfounded, he rejoins the others.

Jaz is speaking. 'Tell me, Stephen. Are your heads in constant touch with each other? Or is there some kind of ubermensch mega-head processing the data?'

'There are many heads. Each aware of the others' activity, responsibilities and experience. Much like the discrete but connected nerve centres of the mammalian brain.'

'What happens to the data? Is there a military agenda?'

'This is a science project. Pure and simple. It's not the scientist's job to police their data once it leaves the laboratory.'

'I think we've had enough,' mumbles Hugo as he swings blithely back onto the ladder, half-climbing, half-slithering down to the next level. Followed by the others.

Another
Hawking
head.

Opening its mouth. Waiting till they are all down.

'Greetings everyone. Most of the robots on this platform are assigned to Advanced Holography. The remainder are with Particle Physics. From here on down, one matrix per floor has a specific module of holographic tasks. Like the one you've already witnessed. In the Burlington Tunnel.' The head floats round the walkway past the robots, all engrossed at their workstations. Its destination is a photo-reactive glass door. Which slides open.

Noiselessly.

'Please come in, otherwise the door won't close and the lights won't activate.' Hugo is the dawdler, still trying to make sense of what he saw above. He enters.

The door slides shut.

Blackness.

And bitter cold.

Gunmetal cliffs.

All around.

A violet luminescence.

Descending. Steadying itself.

Growing and growing

in intensity.

As it grows, so does the noise.
A noise of faraway caterwauling.

Beneath the cliffs stretches an immense plain strewn with myriad tombs and sepulchres. Close together. As far as the eye can see. From each marble sarcophagus the lid has been lifted to reveal a furnace rampaging within. Ragged ribbons and claw-daggers of sulphurous flame, leaping and shooting out in all directions. Convulsing in the violet fog. Screams of guilt. Of shame. Of torment. Of souls on fire. Screeches. Soaring up. Comingling with the brouhaha of their deathless cremation.

'Dante's Inferno,' rasps Hugo,
'the Sixth Circle. Heresy.'

Back to the sliding glass door.
Goodbye to the head.
Down the ladder.

Another head.

However.
Something. Is. Not. Quite. Right.
Syllables sounding, a whole second before the lips speak.
'W-welcome t-to le-le-le-level s-s-s-s s-s-s-s ...'

Jaz aims a finger
at the long droopy ear.
Pokes it. Pokes deep. Deeper.
Her fingertip emerges. From the other side.
'A hologram,' she sighs. But the doyley is real enough, and
trembles when knocked by her receding knuckles.

'Th-the s-speech/image algorithm n-needs m-more work,'
stammers the voice. 'J-just a glitch but we're g-getting there.
What di-di-di-did you think of our African miners?'

'A few glitches there as well,' she clips.

Another door of sliding glass.
Another cold, dark,
deadly, night.

A sound of rain.
Drumming the ground.

Light.
Snaking in.
From somewhere.

An unhealthy gloom.
Corrupting the air.

A barren hillside.

A foam-filled watercourse, spilling into the trench created by its overflow. The consequent meatus is swart and sombre. They follow their bodiless guide through the thickening rain and down the oily slope to where the canal discharges itself, with a relieved splurge, into

a malodorous swamp.

Enormous blood-filled hailstones, raindrops grey with filth and a species of dirty brown sleet come streaking through the air. Thrashing into the swamp. A foetid quagmire in eruption. A shifting turbulence of muddied lumps and twisted cylinders, alive with the gesticulating limbs of bloated humans. Writhing. Moaning. In the throes of diarrhoeic starvation. Nothing to eat. Nor to drink. Nothing but swampslime and their own diluted excreta.

'Gluttony,' mumbles Hugo.

Aside from the icy cold and the nauseating reek of shit, the explorers are unaffected by any of this. Seemingly knee-deep in slime and excrement in the middle of an infernal storm, they are in fact completely dry. Their clothes and hair and skin are clean. Their feet shuffle on a smooth hard floor.

The only visitor troubled physically by the hostile conditions is the hologram head. Its hair and its face and its spectacles are caked in dripping shit. 'Okay,' it spatters, leading them back up the boggy hillside to the exit. 'I'm off. You can find your own way down to the next level.'

The head zooms off
in the opposite direction.
Fading. Flickering.
Vanishing.

So.
Back
to the Galleria.
Down the ladder.

To another head.
Past yet more robots,
at work on their consoles.

Another glass door,
sliding open. On cue.
Another dark arena.
More blackness.
More cold.

A dirty mauve moon.
A smudged, rubicund sunrise.
Giving just enough light. An extensive ditch or quarry.
Beneath the unhappy moon toils an unhappy multitude.

Men, women and children Naked and howling. Straining. Sweating. In opposing semi-circles. Heaving gigantic boulders of granite with their ravaged bodies. When the meteors of rock finally crash against each other, the captives return to the start and throw themselves once more with obscene maledictions against another globe of granite, remonstrating over and over, with every angry breath, 'O why do we hoard, why do we squander?'

The writer sighs.
'Avarice. Prodigality.'

Exit.
Again.
Down.

Another
Hawking head.

Hurry on past the robots.
Another glass pane.
Sliding open.

Into
blackness.
Another. Silent.
Night.

'This level, level four,' intones the head,
'is in two parts.'

They wait.
They wonder. What now?

A glimmer.
Overhead. A warm blush of maroon.
A deep ravine. The banks of a turbulent deluge. A steamy expanse of boiling blood. Through clouds of a dingy pinkish fog they descry a vast oceanic warzone. Men and women. Young and old. Naked. Flailing. Frantic. Those near the bank are solitary and knee-deep, forcing down nonexistent foes into the bubbled gore. But most of the condemned are grappling with one another, waist-deep in blood and desperation. Within the torrid central cauldron of the massive river, a flurry of entangled bodies is locked obsessively in cartoon combat. Sometimes below the swell. Sometimes above it. Lambasting each other with heads and fists and feet. Ripping out bloody chunks with their jagged teeth. Transforming the feral core into a putrid torrent, a spluttering, pink-and-crimson casserole.

And above all this.

The Cacodemon.

Swooping and diving.

An eagle-winged, three-headed, wolf-headed harpy.

The torso, unctuous and humanoid. The silken sage-grey skin, disfigured by blue blotches, swollen buboes and tufts of ash-coloured hair. Its three throats bark like dogs. Its six eyes weep blood. Its beards are greased and black. Its belly bulges. Its black arse festers and balloons.

'Pape Satàan! Pape Satàan! Pape Satàan!'
are the grating expletives that issue, issue, and issue again, like larval grit, from its six-lipped warty jaws.

Harrowing back and forth. Without respite. Careening. Slavering. Dripping acidic blood and grub-green drool onto the paranoid combatants. Reiterating its demonic mantra. Its weapons are the claws and talons which scratch, rend and flay at the helpless wretches beneath. Their faces are contorted. Their lips mouth atrocities. But no sound.

Silence. But not quite.
Just the grim, barely perceptible,
hissing and sizzling from the river.

The head guides the four through the ravine and onto a high footbridge, taking them over the gore-flood of hushed brutality, across a sandy tract and then into a modest wood of weirdly malformed trees.

A low threnody of keening voices.
Secreted. Somewhere.
Beyond the trees ?

Jaz and Hugo investigate. No-one there.
Eugène breaks a twig from a nearby branch. A moan extrudes from the tree. A rivulet of blood oozes from the broken stump and trickles down the bark onto the ground.

'This chamber,' expounds the head, 'represents Dante's Circle of Violence. Those guilty of murder or extreme physical violence against others are condemned to suffer everlasting torment in the River of Boiling Blood. This smaller section is the Suicide Wood, where those guilty of maiming or killing themselves are transformed, for all eternity, into the ugliest of trees.'

Jaz is apoplectic.
'Dante, by fucking Christ!
Haven't they suffered enough?'

The tyro draws her close.
'Can we leave, Stephen?' The head nods. Guides them back over the footbridge. Through the blood and violence. Over the blood-spattered river bank.
Through the glass door.

Having established that the remaining levels consist solely of yet more fables of pain and punishment from the Divine Comedy and that there are in fact no complete and living human beings in the whole nine levels of the Science Hub, Q bids the final head of Stephen Hawking a mumbled goodbye and leads his emotionally exhausted friends on their strenuous climb back up the ladder,
back to the start,
the entrance.

Still here.
No change.
The same sign.

THE STANDARD MODEL
OF ELEMENTARY PARTICLES

Passing
the etched glass
schematic. Passing by
the Quarks, the *down*,
the *strange*, the
bottom.

And through
the double doors.

War
     mth.

Protonic
       coin
out of Jupiter.

The gilded
       flakes,
still falling.

    The   air,

             still sweet.

           The bees
         still working
       their insect shifts
      among the flowers.

      The peacock butterfly
    still trying to be invisible.

     The big double doors
       still marked:

19. *Art*

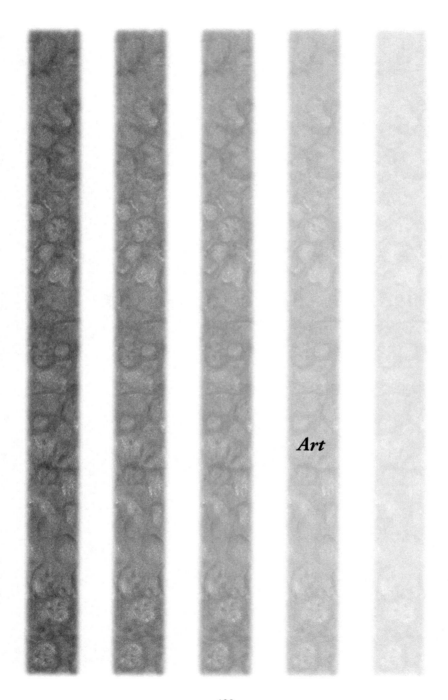

Art

press here   *press here*

A high box-room.

Clad in walnut.

No exit.

They enter.

The doors shut.

A light breeze.

Cool. Sibilant.

Music.

Schubert. *Quintet in A Major.* Bristling through four budget speakers cached in the corners of the panelled ceiling. Q is just unlatching his mouth to speak when the entire opposite wall grinds and slithers up.

Andantino-Allegretto.

Portcullis-style.

Opens.

Opens. Opens.

Onto an exact replica of the R A Schools.

Its stately boulevard.

Its crusty gut.

Spinal

    column.

The same gauntlet of antique casts.

Partially obscured, at the moment, by three armed guards. Tall and broad. Burly as Brixton buses, toting holsters full of black semi-automatic fire-power. The middle one, the biggest, his face riddled with craters, twitches a lip.

'Son of Garth Williams?'

The tyro steps forward.

The guard extends a hand.

'I'm Kevin. This is Bud. This is Frank. Who are your friends?'

Q shakes the hand. Nods to Bud. Nods to Frank. Jaz and Hugo introduce themselves.

Eugène hangs back.

'Tell me, Kevin. My father. Is he alive?'

'He's in charge, but not allowed to leave. Same goes for you, all of you. Having said that we've been instructed to make your time here as… well… as simple as possible.

'Take us to him please. And what the hell is this place?'

'He's teaching. Be free in an hour.'

The Schubert is still playing. Through much better speakers. The fourth movement. In D Major. Theme and six variations. The fifth variation. An undertow of nuances commencing in

B♭ Major, reverting to the title key for the final section.

Q knows it well. Loves it.

Eugène smiles. Dances to the music.

Unregarded by all except Q,

who is also smiling,

also unregarded

by all.

'Have a look round,' says Kevin. 'Just don't do anything stupid. Behave yourselves, we've cameras everywhere.'

Passing between the guards,

they turn left and open the door to what should be the Life Drawing Studio. Smaller and cleaner than Q remembers. The cool light pouring in through the north-facing windows is a little too even. Otherwise all is as it should be.

A model. Male, nude, no jockstrap. Posed on a central dais. Bald and in his mid-fifties. Leaning forward. Weight on his left leg. His right foot raised and laid on a paint-splashed wooden cube. His elbows rest on the bent knee. Around the dais and under the windows are three tiers of wooden benches with rails before them to support drawing boards. All is fresh. Pristine. Polished. The students number a dozen. Equally divided by gender. Most hunched over drawing boards. Two standing at easels.

A sandy-haired teacher is muttering something to one of the students. Q recognises the voice. Horatio Hennes. His old drawing master at Oxford Brookes, long past retiring age, traditional and academic in his teaching, with an unfortunate hare-lip, a quaint earnest manner and a nasal edge to his wheedly voice that was far too easy for his students to mimic. No-one took him seriously back then. His god was, presumably still is, Raphael. He hasn't noticed the group come in, doubtless because he's extremely deaf. The corpse-coloured hearing aids are still parked obtrusively behind each withered ear.

Q wanders over. Sits next to him on the bench, which gets the old man's attention at last. He turns. 'Uh-uh. Hullo. What you doing here?'

'Was going to ask you the same question. I'm looking for my father. He disappeared three years ago but is apparently down here and running this place. Or so says the guard. How about you?'

Happy to talk, Hennes tells how he made some unwise investments with his pension fund, fell into penury and lost everything. He was then offered this job, which came with board and lodging but which, he discovered too late, is little more than a lifelong prison sentence.

The other three disperse and stroll among the students. Jaz is admiring the complex mahogany architecture of the purpose-built studio, with only a superficial interest in the drawings. Hugo is intrigued by the narrow range of styles on display. Very academic. Dry and restrained. Clearly mandated by the geriatric mindset of their teacher. All the drawing sheets have a rudimentary demonstration sketch in the top right hand corner. Eugène pirouettes across the floor to the two easel artists. Stands behind each in turn. Aping with glib panache their haughty, head-held-back faux nonchalance. On the opposite side of the room, Hugo is questioning a pretty young girl of East Asian appearance, who smiles at him politely but doesn't reply. Shakes her head in confusion. Evidently embarrassed.

Hennes divulges that the model on the dais is in fact a hologram. Filmed and processed from a real life drawing session upstairs, in the real Schools. He doesn't even know if the students are aware of it. The advantage of the hologram over a flesh-and-blood model being that the empty clone has no feelings of propriety, doesn't get cramp and can't fall asleep mid-pose. And yes, it's the standard two terms life drawing and one term life painting, even down here. The remaining years are a rigid schedule of painting techniques, bio-chemistry, art history, and learning how to forge from high-res digital photography. And after that?

'They're employed in the so-called 'factory' on a six-year contract, fulfilling commissions from all over the world. Board, lodging and brothel passes included. The guards keep a close eye on them, then it's back to where they came from, I suppose.'

Jaz is restless. Likewise Hugo. And Eugène.
Q indicates that he's leaving. They follow him out into the main boulevard, walking beneath its chain of ornate arches and domed vaulted ceilings, inefficiently lit by the dusty antique chandeliers dangling from the antique nubs of every antique dome. The walls, windows and woodwork are coated in rancid off-white, with a strip of clear transom glass at the top to admit borrowed light from the studios.

They pass under the monumental sculpture of Hercules, hugely muscled and leaning on his club with the skin of the Nemean Lion draped over it. A honey-hued replica of the one upstairs. This one is resin, but the original, explains Q, was cast in plaster especially for the Schools and shipped all the way from Rome in the eighteenth century.

In a glass case opposite stands a polychrome *écorché* nude. Male. One arm raised but mostly missing. As indeed is the penis. Jaz and Hugo are perusing a text pinned to the wall. The silk-sheened effigy was cast from the cadaver of one Ebenezer Jonson, thief turned murderer, executed in 1771.

It was created by William Hunter, the Academy's first Professor of Anatomy, who supervised the removal of skin from the dead body, set the pose, cast it in plaster and then painted it himself in creams and ochres and dark plum. The naturalistic colouring and areas of deep dissection create a powerful, gruesome effect. The penis was removed by Hunter and added later to his scientific collection in a Glasgow museum.

'I'd love to know,' muses Hugo, 'if this so-called teaching-aid, the body I mean, has ever been used in actual teaching. As I understand it, anatomy lessons in art schools these days involve the real dissection of real corpses in real hospitals.' Q confirms that this was certainly the case with his year. And crosses the mall. To the next door.

Life Painting Room.

Pushes it open.

The model, pneumatic and ruddy-cheeked, is seated near the door, posed à la Hogarth's *Shrimp Girl,* in a loose pink-and-grey working dress and floppy grey boater. No platter of shrimps balanced sportingly atop the boater however. She sits hemmed in by the dozen easels and their student appendages, all ostensibly tasked with portraying her in the style of a different old master, cards of whose work are pinned above their canvas.

Jaz and Hugo wander from easel to easel with subtly changing facial expressions, whether of boredom, distaste or guarded approval, is hard to say.

Eugène waits near the door, seated cross-legged and patient, with his eyes closed, on an antique sketching horse.

Q is chatting to an impressive young woman of possibly North African heritage, painting the model full length using the vigorous impasto of Van Gogh's final, difficult years. With some success, in his opinion. Peering down from a black-and-white postcard, Doctor Gachet isn't so sure.

Eugène
uncrosses his legs.
Stands up.

Q takes the hint.
'Time to leave,' he says to Hugo, who has strolled over to eavesdrop on the discussion. Jaz is nowhere to be seen, but then he spots her, sitting on a stool in stilted conversation with a scarred, bruised and discombobulated man in his forties who is faced with the unenviable task of painting a full-length seated portrait in the manner of de Hooch.
He beckons her over.
They leave.

The next place of interest is a cavernous canteen with smeared windows through which can be seen numerous kitchen staff hard at work behind steel counters, with tall-hatted chefs bossing everything from the rear. Giant Monet water-lilies and lithe Matisse dancers queue up around the walls. The pine tables are long and the benches hard.

A salty stench oozes through the doors.

The corridor then takes a sharp right, morphing into a functional, square-section mineshaft with strip lighting, no windows and rough granite walls. Very different from the architecture upstairs, in the real Schools. The double doors at the end are manned by the same three security guards.

As the companions enter they are spotted by Kevin, who hisses a few words into the phone clipped in his top pocket. Force-feeding jobsworth smiles into their blank faces, and with a sarky hint of half-baked ceremony, the guards open the doors and shuffle aside to let in the newcomers.

Factory.

No other word for it. Four rows of open-ended, open-topped, back-to-back cubicles. In two equal blocks. Separated by a broad central boulevard and edged by narrow paths. The ceiling is high as a hangar and crisscrossed by a network of wires and pulley systems.

They are standing at the head of the boulevard. Jaz, Hugo and Eugène meander on down. Every cubicle contains a forgery in progress, attended closely by it's own boiler-suited copyist. A hum of activity. But no-one talking.

At the end.
A bright haze
around a core of faltering density,
from the middle of which emerges a dark blur,
a coagulating cloud. The cloud compacts into a form.
The form becomes human. Upright. Masculine. Walking.
Towards them. The gait, stiff. Brusque but unconfident.
Almost military. But not quite. Lop-sided. And familiar.
Too familiar. The head thrown back
to pre-empt or deflect
ridicule.

An exploded coiffure
of side-combed
curly-crinkly.

Which turns left.
Into a cubicle.

'Wait here,' barks Q, pushing past the others and marching off down the boulevard to where the apparition vanished, followed by Eugène.

The cubicle is empty apart from two stools.

One of which supports the diminished, somewhat grizzled presence of his father. The back is severely bent. The thin legs in their paint-smudged jeans twist around each other like sticks of soiled barley sugar. The skin is prawn-grey. Behind his thick cerulean spectacles the eyes stare out, colourless globes of ash-filled spit.

'What's going on? And what the dickens are you playing at? D'you even know that Mum took her own life?'

'Course I know. I'm sorry about that but it's complicated. Sit down. I'll explain.'

Q sits.

Then stands. Folds his arms.

'Carry on,' he says, 'I'm listening.'

Eugène
slides to the floor.
All eyes. All ears.

'Three years ago it started. Out of the blue I was offered a vast amount of money by a couple of guys who claimed to represent an international money-laundering cartel. They wanted me to make a copy, or should I say forgery, of the Cézanne *Bathers* in the National Gallery. In hindsight I should've been more careful but the money was spectacular. The down payment alone meant I could get out of teaching for good. But I needed somewhere secret and untraceable, somewhere off the grid to produce a decent enough copy of such an iconic work that would bamboozle the so-called experts. They brought me down here. I did the forgery and was immediately put in overall charge. I'm a prisoner I know, but it's well paid, with a luxury flat, plus cooks and housekeepers, and endless perks of the young and nubile variety. But creatively..., I'm fucked.'

This forlorn, shamefaced, decrepit and somewhat dissolute version of his father inspires even less confidence than the previous ones.

Eugène shrugs.
Yawns.

The tyro asks his questions.

Where are the students from? – *Some are from local jails. The rest are foreigners, mostly from police states.'*

Who funds the Science Hub? – *'Never heard of it.'*

Why don't you escape? – *'Impossible.'*

Have you tried? – *'Nope.'*

Eugène rises.
Frowns. Yawns again.
Reaches into his pocket.

Elsewhere.
In the meantime.

Jaz and Hugo have been exploring the studios.
She is interrogating a swarthy professorial man with a huge forehead and a wilderness of fine white hair. With brush in one hand, rag and palette in the other, the copyist is poised before a large painted panel of seasoned hardwood. Leonardo's *Virgin of the Rocks*. Seemingly complete. As in all of the units, one wall is given over to a massive screen on which a digitalised image of the source work is displayed. Introducing herself, she praises the fastidious painting of the hair, the plants and the drapery. He smiles. 'It's taken three months so far but a few more hours should see it finished before being moved to the Drying Room.'

Hugo is hovering in the next studio, standing well back from its occupant, a small short-haired blonde, perched on a stool and busy replicating Vermeer's *Girl with a Red Hat*. The work is tiny. A4 in size, but squarer. Bent over the minuscule panel, she is adjusting a speck in the bottom corner, a spider of chiaroscuro on the carved tulip of a chair knob. The process is at an early stage. The only colours squeezed onto her palette are black, white, and raw umber.

He approaches. Coughs.

She hears him. Turns.

To his surprise her features are Japanese and much younger than expected. The fierce black eyebrows, stony black eyes and albinic make-up present a confusing contrast to her stylish ash-blonde bob.

'Who are you and what do you want?' she demands, in the monotones of an imperious Saxe-Coburg matriarch.

'Sorry miss. Just looking round my new workplace. Hope you don't mind. I'll leave if you want.'

'Well, I do mind. Actually.
Please leave.'

Q's
discussion
with his father
is not going well
either.

'So. You've brought Jasmine along. That was silly. Be good to see her though.'

'She wanted to come. And why silly?'

The shape on the stool
straightens its back.
Looks markedly
less grizzled.

Eugène
seems edgy.
Draws a knife
from his pocket.
Shifts to one side.
For a clearer view.
Concentrates.
Takes aim.
Throws.

The knife misses.
Thuds into the wall.

Stalking across the studio between father and son,
he yanks his blade from the plasterboard wall.
Returns to his position.

Garth is talking but not making sense.

His son isn't listening anyway.

Eugène takes aim once more.

This time the knife finds its target.

Enters the neck, just below the earlobe.

Puncturing the carotid artery.

And stays there.

A bead of blood

rolls down behind the collar.

Garth doesn't notice.

Keeps talking.

Eugène.

Meanwhile.

Has wobbled. Faded.

Disappeared.

Q closes in.

The nearer he gets, the fainter grows the image of the knife and the wound and the trickle of blood. The mordant grisaille of his father's skin appears to be warming up in hue moreover, as he waffles on, incessantly, about Jaz's aunt.

'Belinda was never really my mistress you know. My true inamoratas were always Art and Poetry. There were the occasional infidelities with your mother, and a number of pleasant diversions with one or two exceedingly obliging and most appreciative young models. But that's all in the past. Where's your girlfriend?'

She, by this time, has moved on to a Duccio triptych being forged by a handsome young man of Aboriginal appearance who is describing to her the circumstances of his abduction, exile and training, while simultaneously continuing his job of transferring the map of Duccio's design onto the squared gesso ground of his panel.

Q arrives.
Draws her aside.
Has a quick word.

They return to the cubicle,
collecting Hugo on the way.

But Garth is nowhere to be found.
They ask the copyists in the neighbouring units.
No-one admits to having laid eyes on him.
Several suggest they try his office.
End of the boulevard.

A long, high, wall,
of lavatorial pink.

A wide, high, door,
of varnished mahogany.

Emblazoned
                    across
its top rail,   are

nine
        slug thick
                    letters
of
        the purest
                    palest

                            rose gold

20. *The Office*

The Office

Underfoot.

Slick-fitted. Deep-pile. Aquamarine.

Suspended from the bleached, executive firmament glows an elaborately rococo six-bulb lanthorn of multi-hued Murano glass, beneath which squats an Edwardian desk of polished rosewood, inlaid with lacquered brass curlicues and topped with oxblood leather. And one chair.

Nearby squats a plush-buttoned, bottle-green Chesterfield settee. A magnum of Spanish brandy and three generously filled crystal goblets have been arranged as brash enticement on the oxblood desktop.

And on the wall behind. A transnational library of gaudy art books. All new. All hardback. No expense spared. Each of the other walls contains a door identical to the one they have just entered, either side of which hangs a resplendent yet hideously framed Rembrandt etching. *Christ Presented to the People*. Six different versions. Q is admiring the blackest. The best. The final version.

High above the picture rail. A frieze of twenty four split-screen surveillance monitors, eight per wall, one per studio. The images are split in half. In the first half, whatever detail of the relevant source picture is currently showing on the studio walls. In the second, an aerial view of each unit.

A buzzer sounds.

The on-screen copyists interrupt their work, and shamble with varying degrees of speed and zeal out of their cubicles. Breakfast time.

Jaz walks
over to the desk.
Sniffs at the brandies.
Nods approvingly. Hands them out. 'Viva Van Rijn!' Laughing, unsure, they clink goblets. Swirl the ambrous distillation around and around the crystal pericardia.
Take a sniff.
A sip.

Behind them.
The door. Still unshut.

Q eases it to,
with his free hand.

And waits.
For the click.

* * *

The Office,
is no more.

The goblets
are still in their hands.

But the trio are sunk
in a measureless desert
of fine yellow sand.

A giant sun quivers down
from a cobalt sky.

Petrified,
they look around.
The only object on the desert floor,
apart from themselves, is standing before them,
in the very place occupied just now by the antique desk.
A wrought-iron umbrella rack
containing three parasols.

Hugo,
the nearest,
reaches out for one.
The whole contraption
crumbles to dust. Melts
into sand.

For the two men
the heat is unbearable.
For Jaz, it's hot, but not too hot,
but turning to face the ferocious sun,
even she has to twist away.

They gulp
their brandies.
Bury the goblets.
Remove their anoraks.
Knot the sleeves round their waists.

There follows a brief and inconclusive discussion,
in the furnace of the desert, about their
sudden, bewildering change
of circumstance.

Shielding their eyes against the glare, they try to discern,
or construct, something, anything, out of the shimmering,
horizon-blocking wall of haze. 'Which way?' wonders Jaz. Q
starts to walk in the direction he happens to be facing, with
the sun directly overhead.

Their feet force themselves
through the crazy, painful, desert.
It seems deliberately to be pulling them back, and under.
Sweat pours from their faces. The men untie their anoraks,

holding and spreading them out over their heads as surrogate parasols. Jaz drags hers behind, in the sand, causing Hugo to trip and fall. The oven-baked grit scalds his face and his hands. Impels a metallic croak from his chest.

He scrambles to his feet. She apologises.

He rubs the sand from his eyes.

They slog on. The desert becomes undulant. Changes to dunes. From the summit of one of these, Q descries, some way ahead, a glassy sparkle, edged by palm trees and a lick of greenery. He points. Motions the others to follow. Having climbed and stumbled down several more dunes, they realise the oasis is no nearer. With reluctance they accept that the scene isn't real. Just an irksome. Predictable. Mirage.

The sun strengthens its assault. Even Jaz is swayed by discomfort to use her anorak for protection. Dunes and more dunes. Up again. Down again. Mauled and cudgelled by the heat, still they drag themselves on.

After scaling the crest of a particularly formidable conus of hellfire grit, they see a movement below. A lump. Arising from the desert floor. Growing to the dimensions of a long coffee table. The table walks. A head emerges, from the front. The legs become human. A naked, leprous individual with a long crinkly beard. And longer. Crinklier. Hair.

Crawling up the dune towards them. His beard trails in the sand. As he passes, his face turns up.
Stares at them with tearful eyes.
Something familiar.
About the hair.

Garth?
Nebuchadnezzar?
Deuteronomy Smythe?
The enigma vanishes.

Their infernal hike through the heat and the sand continues for another hour until they come to a long shallow valley winding slowly and darkly through the desert.
'A wadi,' rasps Hugo.

Staggering down to the valley floor, they drop to their knees, scooping out handfuls of the wet sand. The deeper they dig the wetter it gets. Half a metre down, water begins seeping into their small pit. They take turns in drinking the brackish liquid. Take turns in splashing it over their heads.

Cool.
Cooling. Cooled.
In marginally improved fettle,
they raise themselves and follow the course of the wadi until it flattens into the topography of the surrounding desert.

The sun drops two more notches, offering the welcome prospect of a slightly less uncomfortable evening.

To their left, through the haze, they catch sight of what appears to be a group of small pyramids with a larger, lumpier structure a little further on. They alter course and trudge on towards this first real sign of human activity. Drawing closer, they see that the pyramids, five in total, are no bigger than a two-storey house and have been positioned in a quincunx. One at each corner of a fifty metre square. With the fifth in the exact centre.

Beyond this, the larger edifice, twice the height of the pyramids, is taking shape as the back end of a human-headed sphynx. Through the quincunx of pyramids they file. And out the other side. Reaching the sphynx, passing under the ochres of its leonine body and tucked-in legs, the tyro recalls that the head perched on the lion shoulders should typically be the portrait of a pharaoh.

He strains back his neck. Squints up.
Sure enough, the mane luxuriating from the limestone skull has the all too familiar crinkly/curly silhouette. Along with the heavy-frame spectacles, that can mean only one thing. He walks up to the leading leg. Extends a hand. 'Not a hologram,' he mutters as his fingers rub with disgust against the sand-sprinkled stone of his father's clawed paw.

In total confusion and followed by his friends, Q lurches away from the obscene monolith, trying hard not to look back at the features of his father, enlarged so grotesquely.

Despite the ever-slipping sun and the lengthening shadow of the sphynx, the desert is still hot and fiercely inhospitable. The heat haze however has lifted just enough to reveal, less than half a mile away, the white stone walls and arched gateway of a hacienda or small pueblo.

A breeze has sprung up in the meantime, garnering strength and gusting a fog of fine grit into their faces. Fearing a sandstorm, they push on towards the walled village. Onward through the ridged dunes and swirling dust to the archway of white stone. By the time they reach it, the sun has vanished, the blue sky has transformed to a turgid khaki and all three have pulled their anoraks tightly down over their eyes to keep out the stinging grit.

The gates are being rammed shut against the rising tempest by two youths dressed in loose blue tunics and with indigo scarves wrapped around their faces. The trio enter just in time, glancing up at the words carved into the stone lintel:

A La Caja De Joyas

They stop for a breather. Look around.

The village is subjugated by a grandiose, white-and-grey stone mansion of unadorned Palladian severity. A few smaller, chunkier buildings, also in white-and-grey, are spaced out equidistantly in the spacious gully that runs between the mansion and the perimeter wall.

Several inhabitants are racing about in a kind of measured frenzy, seeking shelter from the blast. Dressed in blue tunics. Their brown faces ninety per cent covered by indigo veils or headscarves.

'Tuaregs,' remarks Jaz, noting that the entire settlement is built not of the usual limestone blocks or limewashed bricks but, oddly enough, of blue-veined Carrara marble.

Nonplussed, they start scurrying round the mansion walls, searching for an entrance. On their way they pass a fenced enclosure holding maybe thirty camels, all seated and utterly unmoved by the angry waves of sand-filled air buffeting the pueblo. Then. At last. A narrow door in the blank wall.
Blown open, half an inch, on its sprung hinges.

They squeeze inside, away
from the hot, black,
blizzard.

Into a cool, airy ante-room, with lofty porthole windows
and flat white walls. And a marble floor,
of the deepest, darkest,
blood-crimson.

And another indigo Tuareg.
Sweeping sand from the marble slabs.
Unsettled by the ivory flecks and veins
in the polished body of the stone.
Taking scant notice
of the arrivals.

Opposite.

Another door.

     Another portal.

        Another carved

           inscription

21. *La Caja De Joyas*

La Caja De Joyas

Sugar.

Gelatin.

Corn starch.

Carved-and-gilded.
Paradisiacal. Alhambran. An entrance lobby.
A close-knit squad of sweet-smelling Polynesian moai.
Monster jelly babies. Limestone grey. Rhombohedral.
Shoulder-high. But jelly babies. Differing subtly in pose. All
hyper-spectacled and with the same crinkled coiffure. Starch
from the confectionery process rubs off on their clothes as the
three humans wriggle through.

Out and into a lofty, domed, delicately powdered rotunda.
With an inward-spiralling, down-sloping passageway.
Sentinelled by five more jelly babies. Massive. Monolithic.
Cribbed worldwide from dead or dying cultures. And far
below. At the nadiral hub. A stepped red podium. On which
sits a red velvet sofa. On which reclines. A red-dressed.
Motionless. Man-thing.

The helical trek to the centre takes them down through a
trench of creamy calcitic marble. The quintet of laughably
hyperbolic jellied ikons have been erected at half-furlong
intervals on its low, wide, wall.

The first, dyed orange. Inscribed *Bumper Löwenmensch*. Even from below, the Aurignacian lion-man's zoomorphic physiognomy, its creepily crinkled mane and ponderous spectacles are unmistakable.

Next semicircle. Another gelatin colossus. Pallid vermilion. *Baby Bonny Venus of Willendorf.* Magnified from an egg-shaped, big-breasted, Palaeolithic fertility goddess, even this repulsive caricature has its shock of crinkly/curly and its humungous spectacles, attached congenitally to its tiny, golfball head.

Another sloping semicircle. Another gigantic jelly baby. *Bigheart Urfa Man.* Exuberantly purple, this blackcurrant Neolithic buggaboo is sliced off just below the knee. Again the specs. Again the crinkly/curly.

And now, *Boofuls Gudea.* Ten handsome metres of full-length Mesopotamian king. Top to toe in lime green. Third Millennium BCE. Again the specs. Again the crinkly/curly.

And finally. *Bubbles Nefertiti.* Cast in yellow and finished with the same dusting of sugary starch, this elegant bust is surprisingly bereft of spectacles. The inverted cone of the Nefertiti cap-crown has however been modelled into an ingenious rendition of the all-too-familiar hairstyle.

A sound.

An echoic crackle.

An amplified, reverberant rattle.

A voice …

'Now-ow-ow. Now-ow-ow.'

… the tyro's father.

Jaz reaches for her lover's hand.

Hugo freezes.

Before them.

The red sofa. On its red podium.

On the sofa. Its crimson, silk-suited overlord.

Scanning the newcomers with wry condescension.

Q is baffled.

His father appears younger than the addled mess confronted in the forging studio. The dead-grey hair has regained much of its youthful Siennese richness. The blood has returned to those long cheeks. The head is thrown back, as of old, in its attitude of defensive, wary arrogance.

'You despise me, young Quasimodo.' The volume is lower, but the echo remains. 'Please. Please. No objections. Don't you recall? I said we'd see the truth dawn together. It's break of day above. Here we are below. Time for truth.'

There follows a tedious, fustian diatribe of self-validation, which crawls at long last to its conclusion. 'See life as it is, dear boy. You made it not, no more than I. Take it as it is say I. But that's not robust enough for you. Albeit you'll get near nothing for your pains. I know the kind of living I desire, what suits my disposition, what brings out the best in me and bears me ample fruit by way of power, pleasure and length of hedonistic life. I don't and never will acknowledge that I fail in any of your young manhood's lofty legislations. Continue despising me, as I'm sure you will, but I'm the one up here. Installed on the Throne of Law. With his head held aloft. With his finger on the magic button.'

Unable to contain herself any longer, Jaz strides angrily to the red podium and bounds up the steps towards its leering, supercilious resident. Q runs after her.

A shot explodes.
She spins round on the top step.
And falls tumbling down onto the powdery floor, cursing and clutching her shoulder. Q drops to her side.
No blood. No damage to her anorak.

He looks up.
The three armed guards are in the lobby above, emerging from behind the gelatin moai. One of them has a rifle pointed in

their direction. They vault over the gulley walls and close in on the shocked centre, arriving in seconds.

'What the fuck you doing?' splutters Hugo. Kevin has the rifle under his arm and an unruffled expression on his face. 'The bullets are sponge-tipped,' he smirks. 'A small bruise is all she'll get. Okay?'

Q helps her sit up. 'Does it hurt?' She shakes her head.

From behind. A burst of laughter.
Raucous, then fading away.
They pivot round.

No Garth. No sofa.
Hugo dashes up the steps.
Peers over the rim of a dark well.
Joined by Q. Then Jaz.
They stare down.
A black crater.

More laughter. Just the guards, chatting and joking and ambling lazily back up through the gulley, back towards the nonsensical grove of Polynesian jelly babies.

Then, a juddering,
a rumble…

The sofa,

minus Garth,

arises from its netherworld.

Clicks itself back into place on the podium.

On the nose of each upholstered armrest is a brass button.

Heaped in the middle of the velvet seat are three bags of

breakfast and three bottles of springwater.

'Aaaah,' sighs Q, settling himself on the sofa, crunching into

an egg and bacon baguette. Jaz grabs a bag and a bottle.

Drinks some water. Deposits herself on his lap.

Hugo unwraps the remaining baguette.

Squeezes into the remaining space.

Jaz is first to finish.

Feels around for

the button…

finds it

22.   The Racks

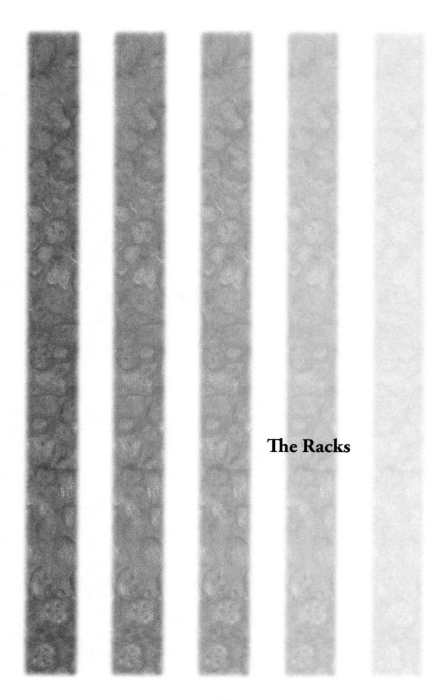

The Racks

down

into silence
smoothly
down
and
d
o
w
n

un
    til
it
    slows,
and stops.

The air.
Viscous. Spiced with oxidising linseed.
Blink-blinking open their eyes. They stand.
Take stock.

A custom-built commercial warehouse.
Two dozen separate drying units. Arranged both sides of
a concrete boulevard. At the far end. More doors. Above.
Another high ceiling. Cross-hatched by another network of
wires and pulley systems.

They enter the boulevard, meandering among the racks. Each rack inhabits its own open-ended cubicle, with its own set of steel jaws, clamped top-and-bottom around its own oil-painted forgery. The units are long and narrow yet still wide enough for up to five visitors at a time to eyeball in comfort the finished commissions.

The fakes are huge.
Even the smallest, Constable's *Sketch for Hadleigh Castle*, is one of his famed six-footers. The biggest is Rembrandt's *Night Watch*. There is nonetheless room enough in the racks for paintings of twice that size if required. The craftsmanship isn't bad, the young tyro is thinking as he strolls with Jaz and Hugo past one of his favourite Titians and on to the end of the warehouse, where she is much taken with a fine Canaletto. *Regatta on the Grand Canal, Venice.*
She slips inside the unit
for a closer look.

Brushing breadcrumbs from his stubble, Q retraces his steps back to *The Flaying of Marsyas*, along with Hugo, who wants another look at *The Night Watch*. After talking to his friend about the history of Rembrandt's picture, how it was savagely cropped by bureaucrats to slot between a pair of fancy columns in Amsterdam's newly built Town Hall, he crosses the boulevard to see the Titian.

The skill of the artisan in mimicking the flicks and daubs of the octogenarian's brushwork is beyond question, but the sheer inability to convey the zeal which knits together the whole crazily psychotic confection is just as expected. He is examining the lower edge. A tiny beaver-like dog is lapping up blood from the strung-upside-down, semi-human, semi-flayed corpse, of Marsyas, the Musician.

But.
A voice.
Two voices.

Jaz.
In contention.
With a man. His father.

Tailed by Hugo,
Q propels himself
stride on bitter stride
down to the far end
of the warehouse.

The big Canaletto.
And Jaz. Head thrust forward.
In a corner. Spewing venom at his father,
who is closing in. One hand stuffed in his pocket,
the other reaching out. Towards her.

'This creep, this shithead leech,' she seethes, pinching out the words like pus from an abscess, 'is coming on to me like ten years ago. When I was ill in bed. Same posturing. Same cheap flattery. Same repulsive hands.'

'That's not true. I was merely trying to comfort a distressed child. I really don't need it and I'm not that desperate. Why would I embarrass myself?' Garth takes a long, slow, breath. In and out. 'Believe you me, dear boy, there's never been a shortage of nubile young strumpets only too eager for a roll in the hay with their celebrated professor.'

The son moves in.
Close. Closer. Closer
to the red-faced crumpled father,
sucking in the pungent aftershave,
the oiled-and-dyed chestnut coiffure,
the oblate, magnified zombie eyes,
the immaculate millionaire teeth,
the honeycomb of sweaty pores
on the suntanned nose.

Garth backs away.
Pressurised deep and deeper
into the liquid continuum
of Canaletto's Venice.

Jaz watches, inert.
Hugo lays a quiet hand
on his friend's arm. Q shrugs it off.
Becomes again the vengeful hunchback
on the stone balcony, by the stone buttress.

Lowers his face over that of his father.
Grips him by the collar. Pushes him hard
into the hungry waters of the Grand Canal.

His fingers slip,
aptly, organically, slip up,
in tonic spasm, up the silk lapel,
up the slimy horror of his father's neck,
round the wet, plucked-chicken sinews
of his father's throat.

The Gondoliers and Carnevale revellers look on.
Too involved in their bright Regatta
to take that much notice
of the thrashings of
a drowning man.

The head. Is driven back.
The arms cavort
                    like tinsel, in a tempest.

The canvas caves in.
To accommodate
the back of a
new skull.

The three or four,
or is it five, competing gondolas
steer a diverted course through the silver canal
around a head which has lost its spectacles,
its dignity, its wish to live

*   *   *

the wavelets applaud
the palazzi approve

*   *   *

the blue sky goes about
its usual but always
slightly different
business

23. Exit

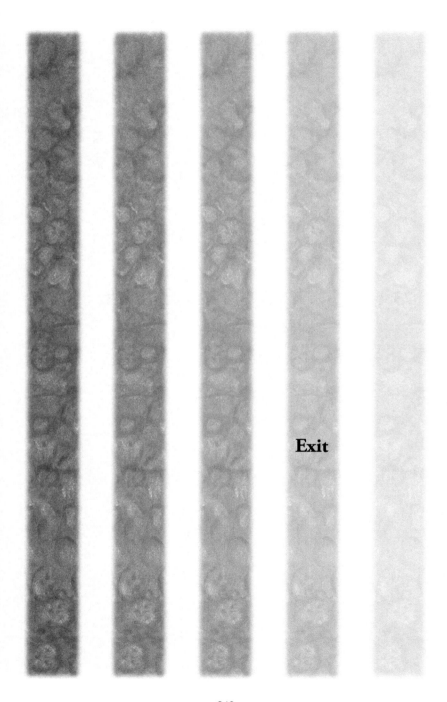

Exit

246

below
the regatta

below the ricin sky
and the dissolute ripples

under the double-doored portico
into a chapel-size service lift

not dreaming drowning
not drowning.

Drowned.

Jaz takes over.
Grips his right elbow.

Button pressed, the lift soars.

The tyro soars, too. Up.
Up through the magma of ten floors.
Up through the penitent centuries.
Passing the inverse declension
of all those rejected,
disgraced
verbs.

The. Lift. Gate. Creaks.

A short dingy walk, to the
Hall of the Great Council.
Past Tintoretto's *Paradise*.

In a migraine dream,
through the Scala d'Oro.
Along the sun-bleached colonnade.

In kaleidoscopes of rubies,
emeralds and early music.
Down the Giant's Steps.

Into the Reynolds Courtyard.
Catching up with Izzy Higgs,
who is also on his way out,
with a small life painting
tucked under his arm.

'Hello you lot. Where've you been? You look awful, Q. And…
oh my goodness… it's Jaz, isn't it? Apologies for that time in
Highgate. I was very, very drunk.'

'Don't worry. It's a very, very small world, that's for sure. This
is Hugo by the way. He's a writer.'

Izzy natters to the writer as they plough along Piccadilly.

The young tyro leaves his Venetian wharf. Chaperoned by Jaz. Through a maze of darting streets. Between high-windowed walls baked biscuit-gold by heat and hubris. Through a glittering, lymphatic motherboard of genius canals. Disoriented. Bewildered. He shakes his head.

'What's happening?'

'Later,' says Jaz. 'We need to go.'

Dropping into the lime-pit of the London Underground, Izzy has already coaxed Hugo into visiting his artsy Camden emporium. Today. Bribing him with lures of secondhand Wagner on vinyl. And builder's tea. And ginger nuts.

The two couples separate.

'We've got your number,' says Jaz to Hugo. 'I'll text you once we've got where we're going, wherever that might be.' She watches inattentively as the writer and the shopkeeper stroll off around a blue-tiled corner.

She takes her
lover's limp hand.
Decides. On Ipston.
His father's old studio.
Tells him. No response.

Tube to Marylebone.

Overground to High Wycombe.

Outside the metropolitan slew, the autumnal tints of fields and distant hills conjure a respite for Q's mangled psyche. Black and white heifers graze in pastures. Scruffy clouds of sheep clump and drift along the hillsides. Within his head, the first April lambs already are bouncing in the April grass, pestering their parents, sending him to sleep.

A sleep of pink and white and pewter.

A sleep of glossy snakeskin reflections.

A sleep of narrow mediaeval passages.

A sleep of patricide.

To the music of Vivaldi.

But which father did he kill?

Disembark.

Bus to Stornchurch. Top floor, front seat.

Sleep again. Taxi. More sleep.

Walk.

Past his mother's house.

Onto the Ipston Common.

Beech spinneys.

Bracken.

Cripplegate.

The burnt-out wooden veranda.

Through the gorsy, nettle-edged pathway.

Into a side door of the brick studio. 'Hope you don't mind,' she says, 'I binned Garth's materials and all his vile artwork, shortly after your mother died.'

Still no response.

Charred rafters. A miscellany of antique wind-up easels, louring over everything. The ambience is that of a defunct Charnel House. 'I'll leave you here for a while, if that's alright. Need to warn my aunt. Won't be long.'

A tight hug. A dry kiss.

She walks out.

He isn't sure

if he's been here before.

So little of his father remains.

Just the black beams and phantasmagoric easels conspiring to destroy all sense of time and place. In a dismal corner, on a chaise longue near the grimy butler's sink, he sees, or thinks he sees, smoking a pipe and talking to himself,

the fugitive impression of Eugène.

And then not.

That's

it.

Find a pen.

Scrap of paper.

Thanks but I can't stay here. Going home. Have to work.

It's the only way. Be in touch. Sorry. xxx

Leave the note.

On a chair.

Up Cripplegate.

Into the Ipston pub.

Order a taxi. Drag himself

through labyrinths of urban murk.

Arrive at his flat in the early hours.

Throw himself on the bed.

Sleep for half a day.

Wake up at lunchtime.

Shower. Shave. Fix lunch.

Camembert and lettuce sandwich.

Plus a banana. Plus an orange. Plus.

An apple. Plus. Two mugs of tea.

Prepare.

The palette table.

Absorb. The live breath of oil paint.

Stand. Once more.

In

  Soho

palette
      knife

brushes

rag

look

look
    again

        step
           back

       look
          again

             begin